ESPIONAGE AND INTRIGUE
IN THE FAR REACHES OF THE
GALAXY . . .

The Lannai operative looked at him steadily for a moment. Her name was Pagadan and, though no more human than a jellyfish, she was to human eyes an exquisitely designed creature. It was rather startling to realize that her Interstellar dossier described her as a combat-type mind—which implied a certain ruthlessness, at the very least—and also that she had been sent to Gull to act, among other things, as an executioner . . .

"You're a clever little man, Zone Agent," she said thoughtfully . . .

AGENT OF VEGA

AGENT OF VEGA

JAMES H. SCHMITZ

SF
ace books
A Division of Charter Communications Inc.
A GROSSET & DUNLAP COMPANY
51 Madison Avenue
New York, New York 10010

This Ace printing: August 1982
Published simultaneously in Canada
2 4 6 8 0 9 7 5 3 1
Manufactured in the United States of America

CONTENTS

AGENT OF VEGA

"It just happens," the Third Co-ordinator of the Vegan Confederacy explained patiently, "that the local Agent—it's Zone Seventeen Eighty-two—isn't available at the moment. In fact, he isn't expected to contact this HQ for at least another week. And since the matter really needs prompt attention, and you happened to be passing within convenient range of the spot, I thought of you."

"I like these little extra jobs I get whenever you think of me," commented the figure in the telepath transmitter before him. It was that of a small, wiry man with rather cold yellow eyes—sitting against an undefined dark background, he might have been a minor criminal or the skipper of an aging space-tramp.

"After the last two of them, as I recall it," he continued pointedly, "I turned in my final mission report from the emergency treatment tank of my ship— And if you'll remember, I'd have been back in my own Zone by now if you hadn't sent me chasing wildeyed rumor in this direction!"

He leaned forward with an obviously false air of hopeful anticipation. "Now this wouldn't just possibly be another hot lead on U-1, would it?"

"No, no! Nothing like that!" the Co-ordinator said sooth-

1

ingly. In his mental file the little man was listed as "Zone Agent Iliff, Zone Thirty-six Oh-six; unrestricted utility; try not to irritate—" There was a good deal more of it, including the notation:

"U-1: The Agent's failure-shock regarding this subject has been developed over the past twelve-year period into a settled fear-fix of prime-motive proportions. The Agent may now be intrusted with the conclusion of this case, whenever the opportunity is presented."

That was no paradox to the Co-ordinator who, as Chief of the Department of Galactic Zones, was Iliff's immediate superior. He knew the peculiar qualities of his agents—and how to make the most economical use of them, while they lasted.

"It's my own opinion," he offered cheerily, "that U-1 has been dead for years. Though I'll admit Correlation doesn't agree with me there."

"Correlation's often right," Iliff remarked, still watchfully. He added, "U-1 appeared excessively healthy the last time I got near him."

"Well, that was twelve standard years ago," the Co-ordinator murmured. "If he were still around, he'd have taken a bite out of us before this—a big bite! Just to tell us he doesn't think the Galaxy is quite wide enough for him and the Confederacy both. He's not the type to lie low longer than he has to." He paused. "Or do you think you might have shaken some of his supremacy ideas out of him that last time?"

"Not likely," said Iliff. The voice that came from the transmitter, the thought that carried it, were equally impassive. "He booby-trapped me good. To him it wouldn't even have seemed like a fight."

The Co-ordinator shrugged. "Well, there you are! Anyway, this isn't that kind of job at all. It's actually a rather simple assignment."

Iliff winced.

"No, I mean it! What this job takes is mostly tact—always one of your strongest points, Iliff."

The statement was not entirely true; but the Agent ignored it and the Co-ordinator went on serenely:

". . . so I've homed you full information on the case.

Your ship should pick it up in an hour, but you might have questions; so here it is, in brief:

"Two weeks ago, the Bureau of Interstellar Crime sends an operative to a planet called Gull in Seventeen Eighty-two —that's a mono-planet system near Lycanno, just a bit off your present route. You been through that neighborhood before?"

Iliff blinked yellow eyes and produced a memory. "We went through Lycanno once. Seventeen or eighteen Habitables; population A-Class Human; Class D politics— How far is Gull from there?"

"Eighteen hours' cruising speed, or a little less—but you're closer to it than that right now. This operative was to make positive identification of some ex-spacer called Tahmey, who'd been reported there, and dispose of him. Routine interstellar stuff, *but*—twenty-four hours ago, the operative sends back a message that she finds positive identification impossible . . . and that she wants a Zone Agent."

He looked expectantly at Iliff. Both of them knew perfectly well that the execution of a retired piratical spacer was no part of a Zone Agent's job—furthermore, that every Interstellar operative was aware of the fact; and finally, that such a request should have induced the Bureau to recall its operative for an immediate mental overhaul and several months' vacation before he or she could be risked on another job.

"Give," Iliff suggested patiently.

"The difference," the Co-ordinator explained, "is that the operative is one of our Lannai trainees."

"I see," said the Agent.

He did. The Lannai were high type humanoids and the first people of their classification to be invited to join the Vegan Confederacy—till then open only to Homo sapiens and the interesting variety of mutant branches of that old Terrestrial stock.

The invitation had been sponsored, against formidable opposition, by the Department of Galactic Zones, with the obvious intention of having the same privilege extended later to as many humanoids and other nonhuman races as could meet the Confederacy's general standards.

As usual, the Department's motive was practical enough. Its king-sized job was to keep the eighteen thousand individual civilizations so far registered in its Zones out of as much dangerous trouble as it could, while nudging them unobtrusively, whenever the occasion was offered, just a little farther into the path of righteousness and order.

It was slow, dangerous, carefully unspectacular work, since it violated, in fact and in spirit, every galactic treaty of nonintervention the Confederacy had ever signed. Worst of all, it was work for which the Department was, of necessity, monstrously understaffed.

The more political systems, races and civilizations it could draw directly into the Confederacy, the fewer it would have to keep under that desperately sketchy kind of supervision. Regulations of membership in Vega's super-system were interpreted broadly, but even so they pretty well precluded any dangerous degree of deviation from the ideals that Vega championed.

And if, as a further consequence, Galactic Zones could then draw freely on the often startling abilities and talents of nonhuman peoples to aid in its titanic project—

The Department figuratively licked its chops.

The opposition was sufficiently rooted in old racial emotions to be extremely bitter and strong. The Traditionalists, working chiefly through the Confederacy's Department of Cultures, wanted no dealings with any race which could not trace its lineage back through the long centuries to Terra itself. Nonhumans had played a significant part in the century-long savage struggles that weakened and finally shattered the first human Galactic Empire.

That mankind, as usual, had asked for it and that its grimmest and most powerful enemies were to be found nowadays among those who could and did claim the same distant Earth-parentage did not noticeably weaken the old argument, which to date had automatically excluded any other stock from membership. In the High Council of the Confederacy, the Department of Cultures, backed by a conservative majority of the Confederacy's members, had, naturally enough, tremendous influence.

Galactic Zones, however—though not one citizen in fifty thousand knew of its existence, and though its arguments could not be openly advanced—had a trifle more.

So the Lannai were in—on probation.

"As you may have surmised," the Third Co-ordinator said glumly, "the Lannai haven't exactly been breaking their necks trying to get in with us, either. In fact, *their* government's had to work for the alliance against almost the same degree of popular disapproval; though on the whole they seem to be a rather more reasonable sort of people than we are. Highly developed natural telepaths, you know—that always seems to make folks a little easier to get along with."

"What's this one doing in Interstellar?" Iliff inquired.

"We've placed a few Lannai in almost every department of the government by now—not, of course, in Galactic Zones! The idea is to prove, to our people and theirs, that Lannai and humans can work for the same goal, share responsibilities, and so on. To prove generally that we're natural allies."

"Has it been proved?"

"Too early to say. They're bright enough and, of course, the ones they sent us were hand-picked and anxious to make good. This Interstellar operative looked like one of the best. She's a kind of relative of the fifth ranking Lannai ruler. That's what would make it bad if it turned out she'd blown up under stress. For one thing, their pride could be hurt enough to make them bolt the alliance. But our Traditionalists certainly would be bound to hear about it, and," the Co-ordinator concluded heatedly, "the Co-ordinator of Cultures would be rising to his big feet again on the subject in Council!"

"An awkward situation, sir," Iliff sympathized, "demanding a great deal of tact. But then you have that."

"I've got it," agreed the Co-ordinator, "but I'd prefer not to have to use it so much. So if you can find some way of handling that little affair on Gull discreetly— Incidentally, since you'll be just a short run then from Lycanno, there's an undesirable political trend reported building up there. They've dropped from D to H-Class politics inside of a decade. You'll find the local Agent's notes on the matter waiting for you on Gull. Perhaps you might as well skip over and fix it."

"All right," said Iliff coldly. "I won't be needed back in my own Zone for another hundred hours. Not urgently."

"Lab's got a new mind-lock for you to test," the Co-ordinator went on briskly. "You'll find that on Gull, too."

There was a slight pause.

"You remember, don't you," the Agent inquired gently then, as if speaking to an erring child, "what happened the last time I gave one of those gadgets a field test on a high-powered brain?"

"Yes, of course! But if this one *works*," the Co-ordinator pointed out, almost wistfully, "we've got something we really do need. And until I know it does work, under ultimate stresses, I can't give it general distribution. I've picked a hundred of you to try it out." He sighed. "Theoretically, it will hold a mind of any conceivable potential within that mind's own shields, under any conceivable stress, and still permit almost normal investigation. It's been checked to the limit," he concluded encouragingly, "under lab conditions—"

"They all were," Iliff recollected, without noticeable enthusiasm. "Well, I'll see what turns up."

"That's fine!" The Co-ordinator brightened visibly. He added, "We wouldn't, of course, want you to take any *un-necessary* risks—"

For perhaps half a minute after the visualization tank of his telepath transmitter had faded back to its normal translucent and faintly luminous green, Iliff continued to stare into it.

Back on Jeltad, the capital planet of the Confederacy, fourteen thousand light-years away, the Co-ordinator's attention was turning to some other infinitesimal-seeming but significant crisis in the Department's monstrous periphery. The chances were he would not think of Iliff again, or of Zone Seventeen Eighty-two, until Iliff's final mission report came in—or failed to come in within the period already allotted it by the Department's automatic monitors.

In either event, the brain screened by the Co-ordinator's

conversational inanities would revert once more to that specific problem then, for as many unhurried seconds, minutes or, it might be, hours as it required. It was one of the three or four human brains in the galaxy for which Zone Agent Iliff had ever felt anything remotely approaching genuine respect.

"How far are we from Gull now?" he said without turning his head.

A voice seemed to form itself in the air a trifle above and behind him.

"A little over eight hours, cruising speed—"

"As soon as I get the reports off the pigeon from Jeltad, step it up so we get there in four," Iliff said. "I think I'll be ready about that time."

"The pigeon just arrived," the voice replied. It was not loud, but it was a curiously *big* voice with something of the overtones of an enormous bronze gong in it. It was also oddly like a cavernous amplification of Iliff's own type of speech.

The agent turned to a screen on his left, in which a torpedo-like twenty-foot tube of metal had appeared, seemingly suspended in space and spinning slowly about its axis. Actually, it was some five miles from the ship—which was as close as it was healthy to get to a homing pigeon at the end of its voyage—and following it at the ship's exact rate of speed, though it was driven by nothing except an irresistible urge to get to its "roost," the pattern of which had been stamped in its molecules. The roost was on Iliff's ship, but the pigeon would never get there. No one knew just what sort of subdimensions it flashed through on its way to its objective or what changes were wrought on it before it reappeared, but early experiments with the gadget had involved some highly destructive explosions at its first contact with any solid matter in normal space.

So now it was held by barrier at a safe distance while its contents were duplicated within the ship. Then something lethal flickered from the ship to the pigeon and touched it; and it vanished with no outward indication of violence.

For a time, Iliff became immersed in the dossiers provided both by Interstellar and his own department. The ship ap-

proached and presently drove through the boundaries of Zone
Seventeen Eighty-two, and the big voice murmured:

"Three hours to Gull."

"All right," Iliff said, still absently. "Let's eat."

Nearly another hour passed before he spoke again. "Send
her this. Narrow-beam telepath— Gull itself should be close
enough, I think. If you can get it through—"

He stood up, yawned, stretched and bent, and straightened
again.

"You know," he remarked suddenly, "I wouldn't be a bit
surprised if the old girl wasn't so wacky, after all. What I
mean is," he explained, "she really might *need* a Zone Agent."

"Is it going to be another unpredictable mission?" the
voice inquired.

"Aren't they always—when the man picks them for us?
What was *that?*"

There was a moment's silence. Then the voice told him,
"She's got your message. She'll be expecting you."

"Fast!" Iliff said approvingly. "Now listen. On Gull, we
shall be old Trader Casselmath with his stock of exotic and
expensive perfumes. So get yourself messed up for the part—
but don't spill any of the stuff, this time."

The suspect's name was Deel. For the past ten years he
had been a respected—and respectable—citizen and merchant
of the mono-planet System of Gull. He was supposed to have
come there from his birthplace, Number Four of the Neighboring System of Lycanno.

But the microstructural plates the operative made of him
proved he was the pirate Tahmey who, very probably, had
once been a middling big shot among the ill-famed Ghant
Spacers. The Bureau of Interstellar Crime had him on record; and it was a dogma of criminology that microstructural
identification was final and absolute—that the telltale patterns could not be duplicated, concealed, or altered to any
major degree without killing the organism.

The operative's people, however, were telepaths, and she
was an adept, trained in the widest and most intensive use
of the faculty. For a Lannai it was natural to check skeptically,
in her own manner, the mechanical devices of another race.

If she had not been an expert she would have been caught then, on her first approach. The mind she attempted to tap was guarded.

By whom or what was a question she did not attempt to answer immediately. There were several of these watchdogs, of varying degrees of ability. Her thought faded away from the edge of their watchfulness before their attention was drawn to it. It slid past them and insinuated itself deftly through the crude electronic thought-shields used by Tahmey. Such shields were a popular commercial article, designed to protect men with only an average degree of mental training against the ordinary telepathic prowler and entirely effective for that purpose. Against her manner of intrusion they were of no use at all.

But it was a shock to discover then that she was in no way within the mind of Tahmey! This was, in literal fact, the mind of the man named Deel—for the past ten years a citizen of Gull, before that of the neighboring System of Lycanno.

The fact was, to her at least, quite as indisputable as the microstructural evidence that contradicted it. This was not some clumsily linked mass of artificial memory tracts and habit traces, but a living, matured mental personality. It showed few signs of even as much psychosurgery as would be normal in a man of Deel's age and circumstances.

But if it *was* Deel, why should anyone keep a prosperous, reasonably honest and totally insignificant planeteer under telepathic surveillance? She considered investigating the unknown watchers, but the aura of cold, implacable alertness she had sensed in her accidental near-contact with them warned her not to force her luck too far.

"After all," she explained apologetically, "I had no way of estimating their potential."

"No," Iliff agreed, "you hadn't. But I don't think that was what stopped you."

The Lannai operative looked at him steadily for a moment. Her name was Pagadan and, though no more human than a jellyfish, she was to human eyes an exquisitely designed creature. It was rather startling to realize that her Interstellar dossier described her as a combat-type mind—

which implied a certain ruthlessness, at the very least—and
also that she had been sent to Gull to act, among other things,
as an executioner.

"Now what did you mean by that?" she inquired, on a
note of friendly wonder.

"I meant," Iliff said carefully, "that I'd now like to hear
all the little details you didn't choose to tell Interstellar.
Let's start with your trip to Lycanno."

"Oh, I see!" Pagadan said. "Yes, I went to Lycanno, of
course—" She smiled suddenly and became with that, he
thought, extraordinarily beautiful, though the huge silvery
eyes with their squared black irises, which widened or nar-
rowed flickeringly with every change of mood or shift of
light, did not conform exactly to any standard human ideal.
No more did her hair, a silver-shimmering fluffy crest of
something like feathers—but the general effect, Iliff decided,
remained somehow that of a remarkably attractive human
woman in permanent fancy dress. According to the reports
he'd studied recently, it had pleased much more conservative tastes than his own.

"You're a clever little man, Zone Agent," she said thoughtfully. "I believe I might as well be frank with you. If I'd
reported everything I know about this case—though for reasons I shall tell you I really found out very little—the Bureau
would almost certainly have recalled me. They show a mad-
dening determination to see that I shall come to no harm
while working for them." She looked at him doubtfully. "You
understand that, simply because I'm a Lannai, I'm an object
of political importance just now?"

Iliff nodded.

"Very well. I discovered in Lycanno that the case *was*
a little more than I could handle alone." She shivered slightly,
the black irises flaring wide with what was probably reminis-
cent fright.

"But I did not want to be recalled. My people," she said a
little coldly, "will accept the proposed alliance only if they
are to share in your enterprises and responsibilities. They
do not wish to be shielded or protected, and it would have
a poor effect on them if they learned that we, their first
representatives among you, had been relieved of our duties

whenever they threatened to involve us in personal danger."

"I see," Iliff said seriously, remembering that she was royalty of a sort, or the Lannai equivalent of it. He shook his head. "The Bureau," he said, "must have quite a time with you."

Pagadan stared and laughed. "No doubt they find me a little difficult at times. Still, I *do* know how to take orders. But in this case it seemed more important to make sure I was not going to be protected again than to appear reasonable and co-operative. So I made use, for the first time, of my special status in the Bureau and insisted that a Zone Agent be sent here. However, I can assure you that the case has developed into an undertaking that actually will require a Zone Agent's peculiar abilities and equipment."

"Well," Iliff shrugged, "if worked and here I am, abilities, equipment and all. What was it you found on Lycanno?"

There was considerable evidence to show that, during the years Tahmey was on record as having been about his criminal activities in space, the man named Deel was living quietly on the fourth planet of the Lycanno System, rarely even venturing beyond its atmospheric limits because of a pronounced and distressing liability to the psychosis of spacefear.

Pagadan gathered this evidence partly from official records, partly and in much greater detail from the unconscious memories of some two hundred people who had been more or less intimately connected with Deel. The investigation appeared to establish his previous existence in Lycanno beyond all reasonable doubt. It did nothing to explain why it should have become merged fantastically with the physical appearance of the pirate Tahmey.

This Deel was remembered as a big, blond, healthy man, good-natured and shrewd, the various details of his features and personality blurred or exaggerated by the untrained perceptions of those who remembered him. The description, particularly after this lapse of time, could have fitted Tahmey just as well—or just as loosely.

It was as far as she could go along that line. Officialdom was lax in Lycanno, and the precise identification of individual citizens by microstructural images or the like was not practiced. Deel had been born there, matured there, become reasonably successful. Then his business was detroyed by an offended competitor, and it was indicated to him that he would not be permitted to re-establish himself in the System.

He had business connections on Gull; and after undergoing a lengthy and expensive conditioning period against the effects of space-fear, he ventured to make the short trip, and was presently working himself back to a position comfortably near the top on Gull.

That was all. Except that—somewhere along the line—his overall physical resemblance to Tahmey had shifted into absolute physical identity. . . .

"I realize, of course, that the duplication of a living personality in another body is considered almost as impossible as the existence of a microstructural double. But it does seem that Tahmey-Deel has to be one or the other."

"Or," Iliff grunted, "something we haven't thought of yet. This is beginning to look more and more like one of those cases I'd like to forget. Well, what did you do?"

"If there was a biopsychologist in the Lycanno System who had secretly developed a method of personality transfer in some form or other, he was very probably a man of considerable eminence in that line of work. I began to screen the minds of persons likely to know of such a man."

"Did you find him?"

She shook her head and grimaced uncomfortably. *"He* found *me*—at least, I think we can assume it was he. I assembled some promising leads, a half dozen names in all, and then—I find this difficult to describe—from one moment to another I knew I was being . . . sought . . . by another mind. By a mind of quite extraordinary power, which seemed fully aware of my purpose, of the means I was employing —in fact, of everything except my exact whereabouts at the moment. It was intended to shock me into revealing that— simply by showing me, with that jolting abruptness, how very close I stood to being caught."

"And you didn't reveal yourself?"

"No," she laughed nervously. "But I went 'akaba' instead. I was under it for three days and well on my way back to Gull when I came out of it—as a passenger on a commercial ship! Apparently, I had abandoned my own ship on Lycanno and conducted my escape faultlessly and without hesitation. Successfully, at any rate— But I remember nothing, of course."

"That was quite a brain chasing you then." Iliff nodded slowly. The akaba condition was a disconcerting defensive trick which had been played on him on occasion by members of other telepathic races. The faculty was common to most of them, completely involuntary, and affected the pursuer more or less as if he had been closing in on a glow of mental light and suddenly saw that light vanish without a trace.

The Departmental Lab's theory was that under the stress of a psychic attack which was about to overwhelm the individual telepath, a kind of racial Overmind took over automatically and conducted its member-mind's escape from the emergency, if that was at all possible, with complete mechanical efficiency before restoring it to awareness of itself. It was only a theory since the Overmind, if it existed, left no slightest traces of its work—except the brief void of one of the very few forms of complete and irreparable amnesia known. For some reason, as mysterious as the rest of it, the Overmind never intervened if the threatened telepath had been physically located by the pursuer.

They stared at each other thoughtfully for a moment, then smiled at the same instant.

"Do you believe now," Pagadan challenged, "that this task is worthy of the efforts of a Vegan Zone Agent and his shipload of specialists?"

"I've been afraid of that right along," Iliff said without enthusiasm. "But look, you seem to know a lot more about Galactic Zones than you're really supposed to. Like that business about our shipload of specialists—that kind of information is to be distributed only 'at or above Zone Agent levels.' Where did you pick it up?"

"On Jeltad—above Zone Agent levels," Pagadan replied undisturbed. "Quite a bit above, as a matter of fact! The occasion was social. And now that I've put you in your place, when do you intend to investigate Deel? I've become casually acquainted with him and could arrange a meeting at almost any time."

Iliff rubbed his chin. "Well, as to that," he said, "Trader Casselmath dropped in to see a few of Deel's business associates immediately after landing today. They were quite fascinated by the samples of perfume he offered them—he does carry an excellent line of the stuff, you know, though rather high-priced. So Deel turned up too, finally. You'll be interested to hear he's using a new kind of mind-shield now."

She was not surprised. "They were warned, naturally, from Lycanno. The mentality there knew I had been investigating Deel."

"Well, it shows the Brain wasn't able to identify you too closely, because they're waiting for you to pick up your research at this end again. The shield was hair-triggered to give off some kind of alarm. Old Casselmath couldn't be expected to recognize that, of course. He took a poke at it, innocently enough—just trying to find out how far Deel and company could be swindled."

She leaned forward, eyes gleaming black with excitement. "What happened?"

Iliff shrugged. "Nothing at all obvious. But somebody did come around almost immediately to look Casselmath over. In fact, they pulled his simple mind pretty well wide open, though the old boy never noticed it. Then they knew he was harmless and went away."

Pagadan frowned faintly.

"No," Iliff said, "it wasn't the Brain. These were stooges, though clever ones—probably the same that were on guard when you probed Tahmey-Deel the first time. But they've been alerted now, and I don't think we could do any more investigating around Deel without being spotted. After your experience on Lycanno, it seems pretty likely that the answers are all there, anyway."

She nodded slowly. "That's what I think. So we go to Lycanno!"

Iliff shook his head. "Just one of us goes," he corrected her. And before her flash of resentment could be voiced he added smoothly, "That's for my own safety as much as for yours. The Brain must have worked out a fairly exact pattern of your surface mentality by now; you couldn't get anywhere near him without being discovered. If we're together, that means I'm discovered, too."

She thought it over, shrugged very humanly and admitted, "I suppose you're right. What am I to do?"

"You're to keep a discreet watch—a very discreet watch—on Deel and his guardians. How Deel manages to be Tahmey, or part of him, at the same time is something the Brain's going to have to explain to us; and if he has a guilty conscience, as he probably has, he may decide to let the evidence disappear. In that case, try to keep a line on where they take Deel—but don't, under any circumstances, take any direct action until I get back from Lycanno."

The black-and-silver eyes studied him curiously. "Isn't that likely to be quite a while?" Pagadan inquired—with such nice control that he almost overlooked the fact that this politically important nonhuman hothead was getting angry again.

"From what we know now of the Brain, he sounds like one of our tougher citizens," he admitted. "Well, yes . . . I might be gone all of two days."

There was a moment of rather tense silence. Then Iliff murmured approvingly:

"See now! I just *knew* you could brake down on that little old temperament."

The Lannai released her breath. "I only hope you're half as good as you think," she said weakly. "But I am almost ready to believe you will do it in two days."

"Oh, I will," Iliff assured her, "with my shipload of specialists." He stood up and looked down at her unsmiling. "So now if you'll give me the information you gathered on those top biopsychologists in Lycanno, I'll be starting."

She nodded amiably. "There are two things I should like to ask you though, before you go. The one is—why have you been trying to probe through my mind-shields all evening?"

"It's a good thing to find out as much as you can about the people you meet in this business," Iliff said without embarrassment. "So many of them aren't really nice. But your shields are remarkably tough. I got hardly any information at all."

"You got nothing!" she said flatly, startled into contradiction.

"Oh, yes. Just a little—when you were giving me that lecture about the Lannai being a proud people and not willing to be protected, and all that. For a moment there you were off guard—"

He brought the captured thought slowly from his mind: the picture of a quiet, dawnlit city—seas of sloping, ivory-tinted roofs, and towers slender against a flaming sky.

"That is Lar-Sancaya the Beautiful—my city, my home-planet," Pagadan said. "Yes, that was my thought. I remember it now!" She laughed. "You *are* a clever little man, Zone Agent! What information was in that for you?"

Iliff shrugged. He still showed the form of old Casselmath, the fat, unscrupulous little Terran trader whose wanderings through the galaxy coincided so often with the disappearance of undesirable but hitherto invulnerable citizens, with the inexplicable diversion of belligerent political trends, and the quiet toppling of venal governments. A space-wise, cynical, greedy but somehow ridiculous figure. Very few people ever took Casselmath seriously.

"Well, for one thing that the Lannai are patriots," he said gloomily. "That makes them potentially dangerous, of course. On the whole, I'm rather glad you're on our side."

She grinned cheerfully. "So am I—on the whole. But now, if you'll forgive a touch of malice, which you've quite definitely earned, I'd like the answer to my second question. And that is—what sent that little shock through your nerves when I referred to Tahmey's probable connection with the Ghant Spacers a while ago?"

Old Casselmath rubbed the side of his misformed nose reflectively.

"It's a long, sad story," he said. "But if you want to know —some years back, I set out to nail down the boss of that outfit, the great U-1, no less. That was just after the Confederacy managed to break up the Ghant fleet, you remember— Well, I finally thought I'd got close enough to him to try a delicate probe at his mind—ugh!"

"I gather you bounced."

"Not nearly fast enough to suit me. The big jerk knew I was after him all the time, and he'd set up a mind-trap for me. Mechanical and highly powered. I had to be helped out of it, and then I was psychoed for six months before I was fit to go back to work.

"That was a long time ago," Casselmath concluded sadly. "But when it comes to U-1, or the Ghant Spacers, or anything at all connected with them, I've just never been the same since."

Pagadan studied her shining nails and smiled sweetly.

"Zone Agent Iliff, I shall bring you the records you want—and you may then run along. From now on, of course, I know exactly what to do to make you *jump*."

He sat bulky and expressionless at his desk, raking bejeweled fingers slowly through his beard—a magnificent, fan-shaped beard, black, glossy and modishly curled. His eyes were as black as the beard but so curiously lusterless he was often thought to be blind.

For the first time in a long, long span of years, he was remembering the meaning of fear.

But the alien thought had not followed him into the Dome —at least, he could trust his protective devices here. He reached into a section of the flowing black outer garments he wore, and produced a silvery, cone-shaped device. Placing the little amplifier carefully on the desk before him, he settled back in his chair, crossed his hands on his large stomach and half closed his eyes.

Almost immediately the recorded nondirectional thought impulses began. So faint, so impersonal, that even now when he could study their modified traces at leisure, when they did not fade away the instant his attention turned to them, they defied analysis except of the most general kind. And yet the unshielded part of his mind had responded to them, automatically and stupidly, for almost an hour before he realized—

Long enough to have revealed—almost anything!

The gems on his hand flashed furious fire as he whipped

the amplifier off the desk and sent it smashing against the wall of the room. It shattered with a tinny crackle and dropped to the floor where a spray of purple sparks popped hissing from its crumpled surfaces and subsided again. The thought-impulses were stilled.

The black-bearded man glared down at the broken amplifier. Then, by almost imperceptible degrees, his expression began to change. Presently, he was laughing silently.

No matter how he had modified and adapted this human brain for his purpose, it remained basically what it had been when he first possessed himself of it. Whenever he relaxed his guidance, it reverted automatically to the old levels of emotional reaction.

He had forced it to develop its every rudimentary faculty until its powers were vastly superior to those of any normal member of its race. No ordinary human being, no matter how highly gifted, could be the equal of one who had had the advantage of becoming host-organism to a parasitizing Ceetal. Not even he, the Ceetal, himself was in any ordinary way the equal of this hypertrophied human intellect—he only controlled it. As a man controls a machine he has designed to be enormously more efficient than himself.

But if he had known the human breed better, he would have selected a more suitable host from it, to begin with. At its best, this one had been a malicious mediocrity; and its malice only expanded with its powers so that, within the limits he permitted, it now used the mental equipment of a titan to pamper the urges of an ape. A scowling moron who, on the invisible master's demand, would work miracles! Now, at the first suggestion that its omnipotence might be threatened, it turned guilt-ridden and panicky, vacillating between brute fright and brute rages.

Too late to alter that—he was linked to his slave for this phase of his life-cycle. For his purposes, the brute was at any rate adequate, and it often amused him to observe its whims. But for the new Ceetals—for those who would appear after his next Change—he could and would provide more suitable havens.

One of them might well be the spy who had so alarmed

his human partner. The shadowy perfection of his mental attack in itself seemed to recommend him for the role.

Meanwhile, however, the spy still had to be caught.

In swift waves of relaxation, the Ceetal's influence spread through the black-bearded man's body and back into the calming brain. His plan was roughly ready, the trap for the spy outlined, but his human thought-machine was infinitely better qualified for such work.

Controlled now, its personal fears and even the memory of them neutralized, it took up the problem *as* a problem —swept through it, clarifying, developing, concluding:

It was quite simple. The trap for this spy would be baited with the precise information he sought. On Gull, meanwhile, Tahmey remained as physical bait for the other spy, the first one—the nonhuman mind which had escaped by dint of the instantaneous shock-reflex that plucked it from his grasp as he prepared to close in. That the two were collaborating was virtually certain, that both were emissaries of the Confederacy of Vega was a not too unreasonable conjecture. No other organization suspected of utilizing combat-type minds of such efficiency was also likely to be interested in the person of Tahmey.

He was not, of course, ready to defy the Confederacy as yet—would not be for some time. A new form of concealment for Tahmey might therefore be necessary. But with the two spies under control, with the information extracted from them, any such difficulties could easily be met.

The black-bearded man's hands began to move heavily and unhurriedly over the surface of the desk, activating communicators and recorders.

The plan took shape in a pattern of swift, orderly arrangements.

Four visitors were waiting for him when he transferred himself to the principal room of the Dome—three men and a woman of the tall handsome Lycannese breed. The four faces turning to him wore the same expression, variously modified, of arrogant impatience.

These and a few others, to all of whom the black-bearded

man was known simply as the Psychologist, had considered themselves for a number of years to be the actual, if unknown, rulers of the Lycannese System. They were very nearly right.

At his appearance, two of them began to speak almost simultaneously.

But they made no intelligible sound.

Outwardly, the black-bearded man had done nothing at all. But the bodies of the four jerked upright in the same instant, as if caught by a current of invisible power. They froze into that attitude, their faces twisted in grotesque terror, while his heavy-lidded, sardonic eyes shifted from one to the other of them.

"Must it always affect you like *that*," he said in friendly reproach, "to realize what I actually am? Or do you feel guilty for having planned to dispose of me, as a once-useful inferior who can no longer further your ambitions?" He paused and studied them again in turn, and the pleasantness went out of his expression.

"Yes, I knew about that little plot," he announced, settling his bulk comfortably on a low couch against the wall. He looked critically at his fingernails. "Normally, I should simply have made its achievement impossible, without letting you find out what had gone wrong. But as things stand, I'm afraid I shall be obliged to dispense with you entirely. I regret it, in a way. Our association has been a useful and amusing one—to me, at least. But, well—"

He shook his head.

"Even I make mistakes," he admitted frankly. "And recent events have made it clear that it was a mistake to involve somewhat ordinary human beings as deeply in my experiments and plans as I involved you—and also that companion of yours, whose absence here may have caused you to speculate. He," the Psychologist explained good-naturedly, "will outlive you by a day or so." He smiled. "Oddly enough, his brief continued usefulness to me is due to the fact that he is by far the least intelligent of you—so that I had really debated the advisability of dropping him from our little circle before this."

His smile broadened invitingly, but he showed no resentment when none of the chalk-faced, staring puppets before him joined in his amusement.

"Well," he beamed, "enough of this! There are minds on our track who seem capable of reaching you through any defense I can devise. Obviously, I cannot take that risk. Your friend, however, will live long enough to introduce me to one of these minds—another one of your ever-surprising species—who should eventually be of far greater value to me than any of you could hope to be. Perhaps even as valuable as the person you know as Tahmey. Let that thought console you in your last moments—which," he concluded, glancing at a pearly oblong that was acquiring a shimmering visibility in the wall behind the four Lycannese, "are now at hand."

Two solidly built men came into the room through the oblong, saluted, and waited.

The black-bearded one gave them a genial nod and jerked his thumb in the general direction of the motionless little group of his disposed associates.

"Strangle those four," he said, "in turn—"

He looked on for a few moments but then grew bored. Rising from the couch, he walked slowly toward one of the six walls of the room. It began to turn transparent as he approached, and when he stood before it the port-city of Lycanno IV, the greatest city in the Lycannese System, was clearly visible a few thousand feet below.

He gazed down at the scene almost affectionately, savoring a mood of rich self-assurance. For he was, as he had just now proved once more, the city's absolute master—master of the eight million human beings who lived there; of the two billion on the planet; of the sixteen billion in the System. Not for years had his mastery been seriously challenged.

His lusterless black eyes shifted slowly to Lycanno's two suns, moving now toward their evening horizon. Scattered strategically through the galaxy, nearly a thousand such suns lighted as many planetary systems, each of which was being gathered slowly into a Ceetal's grasp. The black-bearded man did not entertain the delusion that Lycanno by itself was an important conquest—no more than each of those other fractional human civilizations. But when the time came finally—

He permitted himself to lapse into a reverie of galactic conquest. But curiously, it was now the human brain and mind which indulged itself in this manner. The parasite remained lightly detached, following the imaginings without being affected by them, alert for some new human foible which it might turn some day to Ceetal profit.

It was, the Ceetal realized again, an oddly complicated organism, the human one. His host fully understood the relationship between them, and his own subordinate part in the Ceetal's plans. Yet he never let himself become conscious of the situation and frequently appeared to feel an actual identity with the parasite. It was strange such a near-maniac species could have gained so dominant a position in this galaxy.

There was a sudden minor commotion in the center of the room, harsh snoring sounds and then a brief, frenzied drumming of heels on the carpeted floor.

"You are getting careless," the Psychologist said coldly, without turning his head. "Such things can be done quietly."

The small yellow-faced man with the deep-set amber eyes drew a good number of amused and curious stares during the two days he was registered at the Old Lycannese Hotel.

He expected nothing else. Even in such sophisticated and galactic-minded surroundings, his appearance was fantastic to a rather indecent degree. The hairless dome of his head sloped down comically into a rounded snout. He was noseless and apparently earless, and in animated moments his naked yellow scalp would twitch vigorously like the flanks of some vermin-bitten beast.

However, the Old Lycannese harbored a fair selection of similarly freakish varieties of humanity within its many-storied walls—mutant humanity from worlds that were, more often than not, only nameless symbols on any civilized star-map. Side by side with them, indistinguishable to the average observer, representatives of the rarer humanoid species also came and went—on the same quest of profitable trade with Lycanno.

The yellow-faced man's grotesqueness, therefore, served simply to classify him. It satisfied curiosity almost as quickly as it drew attention; and no one felt urged to get too sociable with such a freak. Whether mutant human or humanoid, he was, at any rate, solvent and had shown a taste for quiet luxury. The hotel saw that he got what he wanted, pocketed his money and bothered its managerial head no further about him.

This curiosity-distracting effect, the yellow-faced man considered, as he strolled across the ground-floor lobby, was almost as satisfactory when it was applied to those who had reason to take a much sharper practical interest in any stranger! Two members of the Psychologist's bodyguard, behind whom he was heading toward an open elevator which led to the roof-terraces, had scrutinized him swiftly in passing a moment before—but only long enough to re-establish his identity beyond any doubt. They had checked that in detail the previous day—a Talpu, Humanoid, from a system of the Twenty-eighth Median Cluster, dealing in five varieties of gems—three of them previously unknown to Lycanno. Queer-looking little duck, but quite harmless.

The Psychologist's bodyguards took few chances, but they were not conditioned to look for danger in so blatantly obvious a shape.

The Psychologist himself, whose dome-shaped dwelling topped one section of the Old Lycannese Hotel, was taking no chances at all these days. From the center of the moving cluster of his henchmen he gave the trailing humanoid's mind a flicking probe and encountered a mind-shield no different than was to be expected in a traveler with highly valuable commerical secrets to preserve—a shield he could have dissolved in an instant with hardly any effort at all.

However, so sudden an operation would have entailed leaving a small yellow maniac gibbering in agony on the floor of the lobby behind him—a complication he preferred to avoid in public. He dropped the matter from his thoughts, contemptuously. He knew of the Talpu—a base, timid race, unfit even for slavery.

A secondary and very different shield, which the more obvious first one had concealed from the Psychologist's probe,

eased cautiously again in the yellow-faced man's mind, while
the Talpu surface thoughts continued their vague quick trac-
eries over both shields, unaffected either by the probe or by
the deeper reaction it had aroused.

As the Psychologist's group reached the automatic elevator, the humanoid was almost side by side with its rear-
most members and only a few steps behind the dignitary
himself. There the party paused briefly while one of the
leading guards scanned the empty compartment, and then
stood aside to let the Psychologist enter. That momentary
hesitation was routine procedure. The yellow-faced man had
calculated with it, and he did not pause with the rest—though
it was almost another half-second before any of the Psychologist's watchdogs realized that *something* had just passed
with a shadowy unobtrusiveness through their ranks.

By then, it was much too late. The great man had just
stepped ponderously into the elevator; and the freakish little
humanoid, now somehow directly behind him, was entering
on his heels.

Simultaneously, he performed two other motions, almost
casually.

As his left hand touched the switch that started the elevator on its way to the roof, a wall of impalpable force swung
up and outwards from the floor-sill behind him, checking the
foremost to hurl themselves at this impossible intruder—
much more gently than if they had run into a large feather
cushion but also quite irresistibly. The hotel took no chances
of having its patrons injured on its premises; so the shocked
bodyguards simply found themselves standing outside the
elevator again before they realized it had flashed upward
into its silvery shaft.

As it began to rise, the yellow-faced man completed his
second motion. This was to slip a tiny hypodermic needle
into the back of the Psychologist's neck and depress its
plunger.

One could not, of course, openly abduct the system's
most influential citizen without arousing a good deal of
hostile excitement. But he had, Iliff calculated, when the
elevator stopped opposite his apartments near the top of the

huge hotel, a margin of nearly thirty seconds left to complete his getaway before any possible counterattack could be launched. There was no need to hurry.

A half dozen steps took him from the elevator into his rooms, the Psychologist walking behind him with a look of vague surprise on his bearded face. Another dozen steps brought the two out to an open-air platform where a rented fast planecar was waiting.

At sixty thousand feet altitude, Iliff checked the spurt of their vertical ascent and turned north. The land was darkening with evening about the jewel-like sparkle of clustered seaboard cities, but up here the light of Lycanno's primary sun still glittered greenly from the car's silver walls. The speeding vehicle was shielded for privacy from all but official spy-rays, and for several more minutes he would have no reason to fear those. Meanwhile, any aerial pursuer who could single him out from among the myriad similar cars streaming into and out of the port city at that hour would be very good indeed.

Stripping the vivo-gel masks carefully from his head and hands, he dropped the frenziedly twitching half-alive stuff into the depository beside his seat where the car's jets would destroy it.

The Psychologist sat, hunched forward and docile, beside him—dull black eyes staring straight ahead. So far, the new Vegan mind-lock was conforming to the Third Co-ordinator's expectations.

Interrogation of the prisoner took place in a small valley off the coast of an uninhabited island, in the sub-polar regions. A dozen big snake-necked carnivores scattered from the carcass of a still larger thing on which they had been feeding as the planecar settled down; and their snuffing and baffled howls provided a background for the further proceedings which Iliff found grimly fitting. He had sent out a fear-impulse adjusted to the beast-pack's primitive sensation-level, which kept them prowling helplessly along the rim of a hundred-yard circle.

In the center of this circle Iliff sat cross-legged on the ground, watching the Quizzer go about its business.

The Quizzer was an unbeautiful two-foot cube of machine. Easing itself with delicate ruthlessness through the Psychologist's mental defenses, it droned its findings step by step into Iliff's mind. He could have done the work without its aid, since the shield had never been developed that could block a really capable investigator if he was otherwise unhampered. But it would have taken a great deal longer; and at best he did not expect to have more time than he needed to extract the most vital points of information. Besides, he lacked the Quizzer's sensitivity; if he was hurried, there was a definite risk of doing irreparable injury to the mind under investigation—at that stage, he hadn't been able to decide whether or not it would be necessary to kill the Psychologist.

The second time the Quizzer contacted the Ceetal, he knew. The little robot reported an alien form of awareness which came and went through the Quizzer's lines of search as it chose and was impossible to localize.

"It is the dominant consciousness in this subject. But it is connected with the organism only through the other one."

The Quizzer halted again. It was incapable of surprise or confusion, but when it could not classify what it found it stopped reporting. It was bothered, too, by the effects of the mind-lock—an innovation to which it was not adjusted. The chemical acted directly on the shields, freezing those normally flexible defensive patterns into interlocked nets of force which isolated the energy centers of the nervous system that produced them.

"Give me anything you get on it!" Iliff urged.

The machine still hesitated. And then:

"It thinks that if it could break the force you call the mind-lock and energize the organism it could kill you instantly. But it is afraid that it would cause serious injury to the organism in doing so. Therefore it is willing to wait until its friends arrive and destroy you. It is certain that this will happen very quickly now."

Iliff grunted. That was no news to him, but it gave him an ugly thrill nevertheless. He'd found it necessary to cut his usual hit-and-run tactics very fine for this job; and so far he had got nothing he could use out of it.

"Does this primary consciousness," he inquired, "know what you're trying to do and what you're telling me?"

"It knows what I'm trying to do," the machine responded promptly. "It does not know that I'm telling you anything. It is aware of your presence and purpose but it can receive no sense impression of any kind. It can only think."

"Good enough," Iliff nodded. "It can't interfere with your activity then?"

"Not while the mind-lock keeps it from arousing its energy sources."

"What of the other one—the human consciousness?"

"That one is somnolent and completely helpless. It is barely aware of what is occurring and has made no attempt to interfere. It is only the mind-lock that blocks my approach to the information you require. If you could dissolve that force, there would be no difficulty."

Iliff wasted a baleful look on his squat assistant. "Except," he pointed out, "that I'd get killed!"

"Undoubtedly," the machine agreed with idiotic unconcern. "The energy centers of this organism are overdeveloped to an extent which, theoretically, should have drained it of its life-forces many years ago. It appears that the alien consciousness is responsible both for the neural hypertrophy and for the fact that the organism as a whole has been successfully adapted to meet the resultant unnatural stresses."

Towards the end of the next half-hour, the pattern of information finally began to take definite shape—a shape that made Iliff increasingly anxious to get done with the job. But which showed also that the Third Co-ordinator's hunch had been better than he knew!

Lycanno was long overdue for a Zone Agent's attentions. He should, he supposed, have been elated; instead, he was sweating and shivering, keyed to nightmarish tensions. Theoretically, the mind-lock might be unbreakable, but the Ceetal, for one, did not believe it. It did fear that to shatter lock and shields violently might destroy its host and thereby itself; so far, that had kept it from making the attempt. That, and the knowledge it shared with its captor—that they could not remain undiscovered much longer.

But at each new contact, the Quizzer unemotionally reported an increase in the gathering fury and alarm with
which the parasite observed the progress of the investigation. It had been coldly contemptuous at first; then the
realization came slowly that vital secrets *were* being drawn,
piece by piece, from the drugged human mind to which it
was linked—and that it could do nothing to check the process.

By now, it was dangerously close to utter frenzy, and for
many minutes Iliff's wrist-gun had been trained on the
hunched and motionless shape of the Psychologist. Man and
Ceetal would die on the spot if necessary. But even in its
death-spasms, he did not want to be in the immediate neighborhood of that mind and the powers it could unleash if it
broke loose. Time and again, he drew the Quizzer back from
a line of investigation that seemed too likely to provide the
suicidal impulse. Other parts of the pattern had been gained
piecemeal, very circumstantially.

It was tight, carefully balanced work. However, there
were only a few more really important points left now.
There might be just time enough—

Iliff jerked upright as a warning blared from an automatic
detector he had installed in the planecar the day before,
raising a chorus of furious carnivore yells from the rim of
the hundred-yard fear-circle.

"Two planetary craft approaching at low cruising speeds,"
it detailed. "Sector fourteen, distance eighty-five miles, altitude nineteen miles. Surface and psyche scanners are being
used."

And, an instant later:

"You have been discovered!"

The rescuers were several minutes earlier than he'd actually expected. But the warning gave him the exact margin
required for his next action, and the uncertainty and tension
vanished from his mind.

He snapped a command to the Quizzer:

"Release the subject—then destroy yourself!"

Freed from invisible tentacles, the Psychologist's body
rolled clumsily forward to the turf, and at once came stum-
bling to its feet. Behind it, the Quizzer flared up briefly in

a shower of hissing sparks, collapsed, liquefied, and fused again into metallic formlessness.

Seconds later, Iliff had lifted the planecar over the valley's treetop level. The vehicle's visiglobe was focused locally— every section of the dark little valley appeared as distinct in it as if flooded with brilliant daylight. Near its center, the figure of the Psychologist was groping through what to him, was near-complete blackness down into the open ground. Whether the alien mind understood that its men had arrived and was attempting to attract their attention, Iliff would never know.

It did not matter, now. The planecar's concealed guns were trained on that figure; and his finger was on the trigger-stud.

But he did not fire. Gliding out from under the trees, the lean, mottled shapes of the carnivore-pack had appeared in the field of the globe. Forgetting the intangible barrier of fear as quickly as it ceased to exist, they scuttled back towards their recently abandoned feast—and swerved, in a sudden new awareness, to converge upon the man-form that stumbled blindly about near it.

Iliff grimaced faintly, spun the visiglobe to wide-range focus and sent the planecar hurtling over the shoreline into the sea. The maneuver would shield him from the surface scanners of the nearest pursuers and give him a new and now urgently needed headstart.

It would please his scientific colleagues back on Jeltad, he knew, to hear that the Ceetal had been mistaken about the strength of their mind-lock. For the brief seconds it survived in the center of the ravening mottled pack, that malevolent intellect must have put forth every effort to break free and destroy its attackers.

It had been quite unsuccessful.

Near dawn, in the fifth-largest city of Lycanno IV, a smallish military gentleman proceeded along the docks of a minor space port towards a large, slow-looking, but apparently expensive craft he had registered there two days before. Under one arm he carried a bulging brief case of the openly spy-proof type employed by officials of the Terran embassy.

The burden did not detract in the least from his air of almost belligerent dignity—an attitude which still characterized most citizens of ancient Earth in the afterglow of her glory. The ship he approached was surrounded by a wavering, globular sheen of light, like a cluster of multiple orange halos, warning dock attendants and the idly curious from coming within two hundred feet of it.

Earthmen were notoriously jealous of their right to privacy.

The military gentleman, whose size was his only general point of resemblance to either Iliff or the yellow-faced man who had been a guest of the Old Lycannese Hotel not many hours earlier, walked into the area of orange fire without hesitation. From the ship, a brazen, inhuman voice boomed instantly at him, both audibly and in mental shock-waves that would have rocked the average intruder back like a blow in the face:

"Withdraw at once! This vessel is shielded from investigation in accordance with existing regulations. Further unauthorized advance into the area defined by the light-barrier—"

The voice went silent suddenly. Then it continued, subvocally:

"You are being observed from a strato-station. Nothing else to report. We can leave immediately."

In the strato-station, eighty miles above, a very young, sharp-faced fleet lieutenant was turning to his captain:

"Couldn't that be—?"

The captain gave him a sardonic, worldly-wise smile.

"No, Junior," he said mildly, "that could not be. That, as you should recall, is Colonel Perritaph, recently attached to the Terran Military Commission. We checked him through this port yesterday morning. But," he added, "we're going to have a little fun with the colonel. As soon as he's ready to take off, he'll drop that light-barrier. When he does, spear him with a tractor and tell him he's being held for investigation, because there's a General Emergency out."

"Why not do it now? Oh!"

"You catch on, Junior—you do catch on," his superior approved tolerantly. "No light-barrier is to be monkeyed with, ever! Poking a tractor-beam into one *may* do no harm. On the other hand, it may blow up the ship, the docks, or, just possibly, our cozy little station up here—all depending on what stuff happens to be set how. But once the colonel's inside and has the crate under control, he's not going to blow up anything, even if we do hurt his tender Terran feelings a bit."

"That way we find out what he's got in the ship, diplomatic immunity or not," the lieutenant nodded, trying to match the captain's air of weary omniscience.

"We're not interested in what's in the ship," the captain said softly, abashing him anew. "Terra's a couple of hundred years behind us in construction and armaments—always was." This was not strictly true; but the notion was a popular one in Lycanno, which had got itself into a brief, thunderous argument with the aging Mother of Galactic Mankind five hundred years before and limped for a century and a half thereafter. The unforeseen outcome had, of course, long since been explained—rotten luck and Terran treachery—and the whole regrettable incident was not often mentioned nowadays.

But, for a moment, the captain glowered down in the direction of the distant spaceport, unaware of what moved him to malice.

"We'll just let him squirm around a bit and howl for his rights," he murmured. "They're so beautifully sensitive about those precious privileges!"

There was a brief pause while both stared at the bulky-looking ship in their globe.

"Wonder what that G.E. really went out for," the lieutenant ventured presently.

"To catch one humanoid ape—as described," the captain grinned. Then he relented. "I'll tell you one thing—it's big enough that they've put out the Fleet to blast anyone who tries to sneak off without being identified."

The lieutenant tried to look as if that explained it, but failed. Then he brightened and announced briskly: "The guy's barrier just went off!"

"All right. Give him the tractor!"

"It's—"

Up from the dock area then, clearly audible through their

instruments, there rose a sound: a soft but tremendous *WHOOSH!* The cradle in which the slow-looking ship had rested appeared to quiver violently. Nothing else changed. But the ship was no longer there.

In white-faced surprise, the lieutenant goggled at the captain. "Did . . . did it blow up?" he whispered.

The captain did not answer. The captain had turned purple, and seemed to be having the worst kind of trouble getting his breath.

"Took off—*under space-drive!*" he gasped suddenly. "How'd he do that without wrecking— With a tractor on him!"

He whirled belatedly, and flung himself at the communicators. Gone was his aplomb, gone every trace of worldly-wise weariness.

"Station 1222 calling Fleet!" he yelped. "Station 1222 calling—"

While Lycanno's suns shrank away in the general-view tank before him, Iliff rapidly sorted the contents of his brief case into a small multiple-recorder. It had been a busy night —to those equipped to read the signs the Fourth Planet must have seemed boiling like a hive of furious bees before it was over! But he'd done most of what had seemed necessary, and the pursuit never really got within minutes of catching up with him again.

When the excitement died down, Lycanno would presently discover it had become a somewhat cleaner place overnight. For a moment, Iliff wished he could be around when the real Colonel Perritaph began to express his views on the sort of police inefficiency which had permitted an impostor to make use of *his* name and position in the System.

Terra's embassies were always ready to give a representative of the Confederacy a helping hand, and no question asked; just as, in any all-out war, its tiny, savage fleet was regularly found fighting side by side with the ships of Vega— though never exactly together with them. Terra was no member of the Confederacy; it was having no foreigners determine its policies. On the whole, the Old Planet had not changed so very much.

When Iliff set down the empty brief case, the voice that had addressed him on his approach to the ship spoke again. As usual, it was impossible to say from just where it came; but it seemed to boom out of the empty air a little above Iliff's head. In spite of its curious resemblance to his own voice, most people would have identified it now as the voice of a robot.

Which it was—for its size the most complicated robot-type the science of Vega and her allies had yet developed.

"Two armed space-craft, Lycannese destroyer-type, attempting interception!" it announced. After the barest possible pause, it added: "Instructions?"

Iliff grinned a little without raising his head. No one else would have noticed anything unusual in the stereotyped warning, but he had been living with that voice for some fifteen years.

"Evasion, of course, you big ape!" he said softly. "You'll have had all the fighting you want before you're scrapped."

His grin widened then, at a very convincing illusion that the ship had shrugged its sloping and monstrously armored shoulders in annoyed response. That, however, was due simply to the little leap with which the suns of Lycanno vanished from the tank in the abruptness of full forward acceleration.

In effect, the whole ship was the robot—a highly modified version of the deadly one-man strike-ships of the Vegan battle fleet, but even more heavily armed and thus more than qualified to take on a pair of Lycannese destroyers for the split-second maneuverings and decisions, the whole slashing frenzy of a deep-space fight. Its five central brains were constructed to produce, as closely as possible, replicas of Iliff's own basic mental patterns, which made for a nearly perfect rapport. Beyond that, of course, the machine was super-sensed and energized into a truly titanic extension of the man.

Iliff did not bother to observe the whiplash evasion tactics which almost left the destroyers' commanders wondering whether there had been any unidentified spaceship recorded on their plates in the first place. That order was being carried out much more competently than if he had been directing the details himself; and meanwhile there was other business on hand—the part of his job he enjoyed perhaps least of all. A transmitter was driving the preliminary reports of his actions on Lycanno Four across nearly half the galaxy to G.Z. Headquarters Central on the planet of Jeltad.

There, clerks were feeding it, in series with a few thousand other current intermission reports, into more complex multiple-recorders, from which various sections were almost instantaneously disgorged, somewhat cut and edited.

"She has not responded to her personal beam," the robot announced for the second time.

"Sure she just wasn't able to get back at us?"

"There is no indication of that."

"Keep it open then—until she does answer," Iliff said. Personal telepathy at interstellar ranges was always something of an experiment, unless backed at both ends by mechanical amplifiers of much greater magnitude than were at Pagadan's disposal.

"But I do wish," he grumbled, "I'd been able to find out what made the Ceetal so particularly interested in Tahmey! Saving him up, as host, for the next generation, of course. If he hadn't been so touchy on that point—" He scowled at the idly clicking transmitter before him. Deep down in his mind, just on the wrong side of comprehension, something stirred slowly and uneasily and sank out of his awareness again.

"Correlation ought to call in pretty soon," he reassured himself. "With the fresh data we've fed them, they'll have worked out a new line on the guy."

"Departmental Lab is now attempting to get back on transmitter," the robot informed him. "Shall I blank them out till you've talked with Correlation?"

"Let them through," Iliff sighed. "If we have to, we'll cut them off—"

A staccato series of clicks conveying an impression of agitated inquiry, rose suddenly from the transmitter. Still frowning, he adjusted light-scales, twisted knobs, and a diminutive voice came gushing in mid-speech from the instrument. Iliff listened a while; then he broke in impatiently.

"Look," he explained, "I've homed you the full recorded particulars of the process they used. You'll have the stuff any minute now, and you'll get a lot more out of that than I could tell you. The man I got it from was the only one still alive of the group that did the job; but he was the one that handled the important part—the actual personality transfer.

"I cleared his mind of all he knew of the matter and recorded it, but all I understood myself was the principle involved—if that."

The voice interjected a squeaky, rapid-fire protest. Iliff cut in again quickly:

"Well, if you need it now— You're right about there not having been any subjective switching of personalities involved, and I'm not arguing about whether it's impossible. These people just did a pretty complete job of shifting everything that's supposed to make up a conscious individual from one human body to another. From any objective point of view, it *looks* like a personality transfer.

"No, they didn't use psychosurgery," he went on. "Except to fill in a six-months' sequence of memory tracts to cover the interval they had Tahmey under treatment. What they used was a modification of the electronic method of planting living reflex patterns in robot brains. First, they blanked out Tahmey's mind completely—neutralized all established neural connections and so on, right down to the primary automatic reflexes."

"The 'no-mind' stage?" Lab piped.

"That's right. Then they put the Lycannese Deel in a state of mental stasis. They'd picked him because of his strong physical resemblance to Tahmey."

"That," Lab instructed him sharply, "could have no effect on the experiment as such. Did they use a chemical paralyzing agent to produce the stasis?"

"I think so. It's in the report—"

"You—Zone Agents! How long did they keep the two nerve systems linked?"

"About six months."

"I see. Then they broke the flow and had a *complete* copy of the second subject's neural impulse paths stamped into the first subject's nervous system. Re-energized, the artificial personality would pick up at the exact point it entered mental stasis and continue to develop normally from there on. I see, I see, I see . . . but what happened to the second subject—Deel?"

"He died in convulsions a few seconds after they returned him to consciousness."

Lab clicked regretfully. "Usual result of a prolonged state of mental stasis—and rather likely to limit the usefulness of the process, you know. Now, there are a few important points—"

"Correlation!" the robot said sharply into Iliff's mind.

The squeaky voice thinned into an abrupt high whistle and was gone.

"I'm here, Iliff! Your friend and guide, Captain Rashallan of Correlation, himself. You haven't started to close in on that Tahmey bird yet, have you? You aren't anywhere near him yet?"

"No," Iliff said. He squinted down at the transmitter and was surprised by a sudden sense of constriction in his throat. "Why?"

The Correlation man took about three minutes to tell him. He ended with:

"We've just had a buzz from Lab—they were trying to get back to you, but couldn't—and what they want us to tell you fits right in—

"The neutralization of a nervous system that produces the no-mind stage is an effect that wears off completely within two years. Normally, the result is the gradual re-establishment of the original personality; but, in this case, there can be no such result because all energy centers are channeling constantly into the Deel personality.

"*However*, there's no reason to doubt that 'Tahmey' is now also present in the system—though unconscious and untraceable because unenergized. Obviously, the Ceetal could have no reason to be interested in a commonplace mentality such as Deel's.

"Now you see how it ties in! Whether it was the Ceetal's intention or not—and it's extremely probable, a virtual certainty, that it was—the whole artificial creation remains stable only so long as the Deel personality continues to function.

"The instant it lapses, the original personality will be energized. You see what's likely to happen to any probing outsider then?"

"Yes," Iliff said, "I see."

"Assuming it's been arranged like that," said Captain Rashallan, "the trigger that sets off the change is, almost certainly, a situational one—and there will be a sufficient number of such triggered situations provided so that any foreseeable emergency pattern is bound to develop one or more of them.

"The Ceetal's purpose with such last-resort measures would be, of course, to virtually insure the destruction of any investigator who had managed to overcome his other defenses, and who was now at the point of getting a direct line on *him* and his little pals.

"So you'll have to watch . . . well, Zones wants to get through to you now, and they're getting impatient. Good luck, Iliff!"

Iliff leaned forward then and shut off the transmitter. For a moment or so after that, he sat motionless, his yellow eyes staring with a hard, flat expression at something unseen. Then he inquired:

"Did you get Pagadan?"

"There've been several blurred responses in the past few minutes," the robot answered. "Apparently, she's unable to get anything beyond the fact that you *are* trying to contact her—and she is also unable to amplify her reply to the extent required just now. Do you have any definite message?"

"Yes," Iliff said briskly. "As long as you get any response from her at all, keep sending her this: 'Kill Tahmey! Get off Gull!' Make it verbal and strong. Even if the beam doesn't clear, that much might get through."

"There's a very good chance of it," the robot agreed. It added, after a moment, "But the Interstellar operative is not very likely to be successful in either undertaking, Iliff."

There was another pause before Iliff replied.

"No," he said then. "I'm afraid not. But she's a capable being—she does have a chance."

Description: . . . mind-parasite of extragalactic origin, accidentally introduced into our Zones and now widely scattered there . . . In its free state a nonmaterial but coherent form of conscious energy, characterized by high spatial motility.
. . . basic I.Q. slightly above A-type human being. Behavior . . . largely on reflex-intuition levels. The basic procedures underlying its life-cycle are not consciously comprehended by the parasite and have not, at present, been explained.

Cycle: . . . the free state, normally forming only a fraction of the Ceetal life-cycle, may be extended indefinitely until the parasite contacts a suitable host-organism. Oxygen-breathing life-forms with neural mechanisms in the general class of the human nervous system and its energy areas serve this purpose.

On contacting a host, the Ceetal undergoes changes in itself enabling it to control the basic energizing drives of the host-organism. It then develops the host's neural carriers to a constant point *five times* beyond the previous absolute emergency overload.

In type-case Ceetal-Homo—Lycanno S-4, 1782—a drastic localized hypertrophy of the central nerve tissue masses was observed, indicating protective measures against the overload induced in the organism.

The advantages to the parasite of developing a host-organism of such abnormal potency and efficiency in its environment are obvious, as it is indissolubly linked to its host for the major part of its long parasitic stage and cannot survive the host's death. Barring accidents or superior force, it is, however, capable of prolonging the host's biological life-span almost indefinitely.

At the natural end of this stage, the Ceetal reproduces, the individual parasite dividing into eight free-stage forms. The host is killed in the process of division, and each Ceetal is freed thereby to initiate a new cycle.

CHIEF G.Z.: FROM CORRELATION

F. . . . The numerical strength of the original swarm of free-stage Ceetals can thus be set at approximately forty-nine thousand. The swarm first contacted the Toeller Planet and, with the exception of less than a thousand individuals, entered symbiosis with the highest life-form evolved there.

The resultant emergence of the "Toeller-Worm," previously regarded as the most remarkable example known of spontaneous mental evolution in a species, is thereby explained. The malignant nature of the Super-Toeller mirrors the essentially predatory characteristics of the Ceetal. Its complete extermination by our forces involved the destruction of the entire Ceetal swarm, excepting the individuals which had deferred adopting a host.

G. Practical chances of a similar second swarm of these parasites contacting our galaxy are too low to permit evaluation.

H. The threat from the comparatively few remaining Ceetals derives from the survivors' decision to select their hosts only from civilized species with a high basic I.Q., capable of developing and maintaining a dominating influence throughout entire cultural systems.

In the type-case reported, the Ceetal not only secured a complete political dominance of the Class-Twelve System of Lycanno but extended its influence into three neighboring systems.

Since all surviving Ceetals maintain contact with each other and the identity and location of one hundred and eighteen of these survivors was given in the Agent's report, it should not be too difficult to dispose of them before their next period of reproduction—which would, of course, permit the parasite to disperse itself to a dangerous extent throughout the galaxy.

The operation cannot be delayed, however, as the time of reproduction for the first Ceetals to adopt hosts of human-level I.Q. following the destruction of the Toeller-Worms can now be no more than between two and five years—standard—in the future. The danger is significantly increased, of course, by their more recent policy of selecting and conserving hosts of *abnormally* high I.Q. rating well in advance of the "change."

The menace to civilization from such beings, following their mental hypertrophy and under Ceetal influence, can hardly be overstated.

The problem of disposing of all surviving Ceetals—or, failing that, of all such prospective super-hosts—must therefore be considered one of utmost urgency.

"They're telling me!" the Third Co-ordinator said distractedly. He rubbed his long chin, and reached for a switch.

"Psych-tester?" he said. "You heard them? What are the chances of some other Ceetal picking up U-1?"

"It must be assumed," a mechanical voice replied, "that the attempt will be made promptly. The strike you have initiated against those who were revealed by the Agent's report cannot prevent some unknown survivor from ordering U-1's removal to another place of concealment, where he could be picked up at will. Since you are counting on a lapse of two days before the strike now under way will have yielded sufficient information to permit you to conclude the operation against the Ceetals, several of them may succeed in organizing their escape—and even a single Ceetal in possession of such a host as U-1 would indicate the eventual dominance of the species. Galactic Zones has no record of any other mentality who would be even approximately so well suited to their purposes."

"Yes," said the Co-ordinator. "Their purposes— You think then if U-1 got their treatment, being what he is, he could take *us?*"

"Yes," the voice said. "He could."

The Co-ordinator nodded thoughtfully. His face looked perhaps a little harsher, a little grayer than usual.

"Well, we've done what we can from here," he said presently. "The first *other* Agent will get to Gull in eleven hours, more or less. There'll be six of them there tomorrow. And a fleet of destroyers within call range—none of them in time to do much good, I'm afraid!"

"That is the probability," the voice agreed.

"Zone Agent Iliff has cut communication with us," the Co-ordinator went on. "Correlation informed him they had identified Tahmey as U-1. He would be, I suppose, proceeding at top velocities to Gull?"

"Yes, naturally."

"Interstellar reports they have not been able to contact their operative on Gull. It appears," the Co-ordinator concluded, rather bleakly, "that Zone Agnet Iliff understands the requirements of the situation."

"Yes," the voice said, "he does."

"G. Z. Headquarters is still trying to get through," the robot said. After a moment, it added, "Iliff, this is no longer a one-agent mission."

"You're right about that! Half the Department's probably blowing its jets trying to converge on Gull right now. They'll get there a little late, though. Meanwhile they know what we know, or as much of it as is good for them. How long since you got the last sign from Pagadan?"

"Over two hours."

Iliff was silent a moment. "You might as well quit working her beam," he said finally. "But keep it open, just in case. And pour on that power till we get to Gull!"

It did not take long after his landing on that planet to establish with a reasonable degree of certainty that if Pagadan was still present, she was in no condition to respond to any kind of telepathic message. It was only a very little later —since he was working on the assumption that caution was not a primary requirement just now—before he disclosed the much more significant fact that the same held true of the personage who had been known as Deel.

The next hour, however—until he tapped the right three or four minds—was a dragging nightmare. Then he had the additional information that the two he sought had departed from the planet, together, but otherwise unaccompanied, not too long after he had sent Pagadan his original message.

He flashed the information back to the docked ship, adding:

"It's a question, of course, of who took whom along. My own guess is Pagadan hadn't tripped any triggers yet and was still in charge—and U-1 was still Deel—when they left here. The ship's a single-pilot yacht, shop-new, fueled for a fifty-day trip. No crew; no destination recorded.

"Pass it on to Headquarters right away! They still won't be able to do anything about it; but anyway, it's an improvement."

"That's done," the robot returned impassively. "And now?"

"I'm getting back to you at speed—we're going after them, of course."

"She must have got the message," the robot said after a moment, "but not clearly enough to realize exactly what you wanted. How did she do it?"

"Nobody here seems to know—she blasted those watchdogs in one sweep, and Gull's been doing flip-flops quietly ever since. The Ceetal's gang is in charge of the planet, of course, and they think Deel and his kidnapers are still somewhere around. They've just been alerted from Lycanno that something went wrong *there* in a big way; but again they don't know what.

"And now they've also begun to suspect somebody's been poking around in their minds pretty freely this last hour or so."

The two men in the corridor outside the Port Offices were using mind-shields of a simple but effective type. It was the motor tension in their nerves and muscles that warned him first, surging up as he approached, relaxing slightly—but only slightly—when he was past.

He drove the warning to the ship.

"Keep an open line of communication between us, and look out for yourself. The hunt's started up at this end!"

"The docks are clear of anything big enough to matter," the robot returned instantly. "I'm checking upstairs. How bad does it look? I can be with you in three seconds from here."

"You'd kill a few thousand bystanders doing it, big boy!

This section's built up. Just stay where you are. There are two men following me, a bunch more waiting behind the next turn of this corridor. All wearing mind-shields—looks like government police."

A second later: "They're set to use paralyzers, so there's no real danger. The Ceetal's outfit wants me alive, for questioning."

"What will you do?"

"Let them take me. It's *you* they're interested in! Lycanno's been complaining about us, and they think we might be here to get Deel and the Lannai off the planet. How does it look around you now?"

"Quiet, but not good! There're some warships at extreme vision range where they can't do much harm; but too many groups of men within two hundred miles of us are wearing mind-shields and waiting for something. I'd say they're ready to use fixed-mount space guns now, in case we try to leave without asking again."

"That would be it— Well, here go the paralyzers!"

He stepped briskly around the corridor corner and stopped short, rigid and transfixed in flickering white fountains of light that spouted at him from the nozzles of paralyzer guns in the hands of three of the eight men waiting there.

After a fifth of a second, the beams snapped off automatically. The stiffness left Iliff's body more slowly; he slumped then against the wall and slid to the floor, sagging jaw drawing his face down into an expression of foolish surprise.

One of the gunmen stepped towards him, raised his head and pried up an eyelid.

"He's safe!" he announced with satisfaction. "He'll stay out as long as you want him that way."

Another man spoke into a wristphone.

"Got him! Orders?"

"Get him into the ambulance waiting at the main entrance of the building!" a voice crackled back. "Take him to Dock 709. We've got to investigate that ship, and we'll need him to get inside."

"Thought it would be that," Iliff's murmur reached the ship. "They'll claim I was in an accident or something and ask to bring me in." The thought trailed off, started up again a moment later: "They might as well be using sieves as those government-issue mind-shields! These boys here don't know another thing except that I'm wanted, but we can't afford to wait any longer. We'll have to take them along. Get set to leave as soon as we're inside!"

The eight men who brought him through the ship's ground lock—six handling his stretcher, two following helpfully—were of Gull's toughest; an alert, well-trained and well-armed group, prepared for almost any kind of trouble. However, they never had a chance.

The lock closed soundlessly, but instantaneously, on the heels of the last of them. From the waiting ambulance and a number of other camouflaged vehicles outside concealed semi-portables splashed wild gusts of fire along the ship's flanks—then they were variously spun around or rolled over in the backwash of the take-off. A single monstrous thunder-clap seemed to draw an almost visible line from the docks towards the horizon; the docks groaned and shook, and the ship had once more vanished.

A number of seconds later, the spaceport area was shaken again—this time by the crash of a single fixed-mount space gun some eighty miles away. It was the only major weapon to go into action against the fugitive on that side of the planet.

Before its sound reached the docks, two guns on the opposite side of Gull also spewed their stupendous charges of energy into space, but very briefly. Near the pole, the ship had left the planet's screaming atmosphere in an apparent head-on plunge for Gull's single moon, which was the system's main fortress. This cut off all fire until, halfway to the satellite, the robot veered off at right angles and flashed out of range on the first half-turn of a swiftly widening evasion spiral.

The big guns of the moon forts continued to snarl into space a full minute after the target had faded beyond the ultimate reach of their instruments.

Things *could* have been much worse, Iliff admitted. And presently found himself wondering just what he had meant by that.

He was neither conscious nor unconscious. Floating in a little Nirvana of first-aid treatment, he was a disembodied mind vaguely aware of being hauled back once more—and more roughly than usual—to the world of reality. And as usual, he was expected to be doing something there—something disagreeable.

Then he realized the robot was dutifully droning a report of recent events into his mind while it continued its efforts to rouse him.

It really wasn't so bad! They weren't actually crippled; they could still outrun almost anything in space they couldn't outfight—as the pursuit had learned by now. No doubt, he might have foreseen the approximate manner in which the robot would conduct their escape under the guns of an alerted planet and a sizable section of that planet's war fleet—while its human master and the eight men from Gull hung insensible to everything in the webs of the force-field that had closed on them with the closing of the ground lock.

A clean-edged sixteen-foot gap scooped out of the compartment immediately below the lock was, of course, nobody's fault. Through the wildest of accidents, they'd been touched there, briefly and terribly, by the outer fringe of a bolt of energy hurled after them by one of Gull's giant moon-based guns.

The rest of the damage—though consisting of comparatively minor rips and dents—could not be so simply dismissed. It was the result, pure and simple, of slashing head-long through clusters of quick-firing fighting ships, which could just as easily have been avoided.

Dreamily, Iliff debated taking a run to Jeltad and having the insubordinate electronic mentality put through an emotional overhaul there. It wasn't the first time the notion had come to him, but he'd always relented. Now he would see it was attended to. And at once—

With that, he was suddenly awake and aware of the job much more immediately at hand. Only a slight sick fuzziness remained from the measures used to jolt him out of the force-field sleep and counteract the dose of paralysis rays he'd stopped. And that was going, as he bent and stretched, grimacing at the burning tingle of the stuff that danced like frothy acid through his arteries. Meanwhile, the robot's steel tentacles were lifting his erstwhile captors, still peacefully asleep, into a lifeboat which was then launched into space, came round in a hesitant half-circle and started resolutely back towards Gull.

"Here's our next move," Iliff announced as the complaining hum of the lifeboat's "pick-me-up" signals began to fade from their instruments. "They didn't get much of a start on us—and in an ordinary stellar-type yacht, at that. If they're going where I think they are, we might catch up with them almost any moment. But we've got to be sure, so start laying a global interception pattern at full emergency speeds—centered on Gull, of course. Keep detectors full on and telepath broadcast at ultimate nondirectional range. Call me if you get the faintest indication of a pick-up on either line."

The muted brazen voice stated:

"That's done."

"Fine. The detectors should be our best bet. About the telepath: we're not going to call Pagadan directly, but we'll try for a subconscious response. U-1's got to be in charge by now, unless Correlation's quit being omniscient, but he might not spot that—at least, not right away. Give her this—"

Events had been a little too crowded lately to make the memory immediately accessible. But, after a moment's groping, he brought it from his mind: the picture of a quiet, dawnlit city—seas of sloping, ivory-tinted roofs and slender towers against a flaming sky.

The pickup came on the telepath an hour later.

"They're less than half a light-year out. Shall I slide in and put a tractor on them?"

"Keep sliding in, but no tractors! Not yet." Iliff chewed his lower lip thoughtfully. "Sure she didn't respond again?"

"Not after that first subconscious reply. But the yacht may have been blanked against telepathy immediately afterwards."

"Well, anyway, she was still alive then," Iliff said resignedly. "Give Headquarters the yacht's location, and tell them to quit mopping their brows because U-1's on his own now—and any Ceetal that gets within detection range of him will go free-stage the hard way. Then drop a field of freezers over that crate. I want her stopped dead. I guess I'll have to board—"

He grimaced uncomfortably and added, "Get in there fast, fella, but watch the approach! There *couldn't* be any heavy armament on that yacht, but U-1's come up with little miracles before this. Maybe that Ceetal was lucky the guy never got back to Lycanno to talk to him. It's where he was pointed, all right."

"Headquarters is now babbling emotional congratulations," the robot reported, rather coldly. "They also say two Vegan destroyers will be able to reach the yacht within six hours."

"That's nice!" Iliff nodded. "Get just a few more holes punched in you, and we could use those to tow you in."

Enclosed in a steel bubble of suit-armor, he presently propelled himself to the lock. The strange ship, still some five minutes' flight away in fact, appeared to be lying motionless at point-blank range in the port-screens—bow and flanks sparkling with the multiple pinpoint glitter of the freezer field which had wrapped itself around her like a blanket of ravenous, fiery leeches. Any ripple or thrust of power of which she was capable would be instantly absorbed now and dissipated into space; she was effectively immobilized and would remain so for hours.

"But the field's not flaring," Iliff said. He ran his tongue gently over his lips. "That guy does know his stuff! He's managed to insulate his power sources and he's sitting there betting we won't blast the ship but come over and try to pry him out. The trouble is, he's right."

The robot spoke then, for the first time since it had scattered the freezer field in the yacht's path. "Iliff," it stated impersonally and somewhat formally, "regulations do not permit you to attempt the boarding of a hostile spaceship under such suicidal conditions. I am therefore authorized—"

The voice broke off, on a note of almost human surprise. Iliff had not shifted his eyes from the port-screen below him. After a while, he said dryly:

"It was against regulations when I tinkered with your impulses till I found the set that would let you interfere with me for my own good. You've been without that set for years, big boy—except when you were being overhauled."

"It was a foolish thing to do," the robot answered. "I was given no power to act against your decisions, even when they included suicide, if they were justified in the circumstances that formed them. That is *not* the case here. You should either wait for the destroyers to come up or else let me blast U-1 and the yacht together, without any further regard for the fate of the Interstellar operative—though she is undoubtedly of some importance to civilization."

"Galactic Zones thinks so," Iliff nodded. "They'd much rather she stays alive."

"Obviously, that cannot compare with the importance of destroying U-1 the instant the chance is offered. As chief of the Ghant Spacers, his murders were counted, literally, by planetary systems. If you permit his escape now, you give him the opportunity to resume that career."

"I haven't the slightest intention of permitting his escape," Iliff objected mildly.

"My responses are limited," the robot reminded him. "Within those limits I surpass you, of course, but beyond them I need your guidance. If you force an entry for yourself into that ship, you may logically expect to die, and because of the telepathic block around it I shall not be aware of your death. You cannot be certain then that I shall be able to prevent a mind such as that of U-1 from effecting his escape before the destroyers get here."

Iliff snarled, suddenly white and shaking. He checked himself with difficulty, drew a long, slow breath. "I'm scared of the guy!" he complained, somewhat startled himself by his reaction. "And you're not making me feel any better. Now quit giving good advice, and just listen for a change!"

He went on carefully:

"The Lannai's quite possibly dead. But if she isn't, U-1 isn't likely to kill her now until he finds out what we're after. Even for him, it's a pretty desperate mess—he'll figure we're Vegan, so he won't even try to dicker. But he'll also figure that as long as we think she's alive, we'll be just a little more cautious about how we strike at him.

"So it's worth taking a chance on trying to get her out of there. And here's what *you* do. In the first place, don't under any circumstances get any closer than medium beaming range to that crate. Then, just before I reach the yacht, you're to put a tractor on its forward spacelock and haul it open. That will let me in close to the control room, and that's where U-1's got to be.

"Once I'm inside, the telepath block will, of course, keep me from communicating. If the block goes down suddenly and I start giving you orders from in there, ignore them! The chances are I'll be talking for U-1. You understand that—I'm giving you an order now to ignore any subsequent orders until you've taken me back aboard again."

"I understand."

"Good. Whatever happens, you're to circle that yacht for twenty minutes after I enter, and at the exact end of that time you're to blast it. If Pagadan or I, or both of us, get out before the time is up, that's fine. But don't pick us up, or let us come aboard, or pay any attention to any instructions we give you until you've burned the yacht. If U-1 is able to control us, it's not going to do him any good. If he comes out himself—with or without us, in a lifeboat or armor—you blast him instantly, of course. Lab would like to study that brain all right, but this is one time I can't oblige them. You've got all that?"

"I've got it, yes."

"Then can you think of any other trick he might pull to get out of the squeeze?"

The robot was silent a moment. "No," it said then. "I can't. But U-1 probably could."

"Yes, he probably could," Iliff admitted thoughtfully. "But not in twenty minutes—and it will be less than that, because he's going to be a terribly occupied little pirate part of the time, and a pretty shaky one, if nothing else, the rest of it. I may not be able to take him, but I'm sure going to make his head swim!"

It was going wrong before it started—but it was better not to think of that.

Actually, of course, he had never listed the entering of

a hostile ship held by an experienced and desperate spacer among his favorite games. The powers that hurled a sliver of sub-steel alloys among the stars at dizzying multiples of the speed of light could be only too easily rearranged into a variety of appalling traps for any intruder.

U-1, naturally, knew every trick in the book and how to improve on it. On the other hand, he'd been given no particular reason to expect interception until he caught and blocked their telepathbeam—unless he had managed, in that space of time, to break down the Lannai's mind-shields without killing her, which seemed a next to impossible feat even for him.

The chances were, then, that the spacer had been aware of pursuit for considerably less than an hour, and that wasn't time enough to become really well prepared to receive a boarding party—or so Iliff hoped.

The bad part of it was that it was taking a full four minutes in his armor to bridge the gap between the motionless, glittering yacht and the robot, which had now begun circling it at medium range. That was a quite unavoidable safety measure for the operation as a whole—and actually U-1 should not be able to strike at him by any conceivable means before he was inside the yacht itself. But his brief outburst on the ship was the clearest possible warning that his emotional control had dropped suddenly, and inexplicably, to a point just this side of sanity.

He'd lived with normal fear for years—that was another thing; but only once before had he known a sensation comparable to this awareness of swirling, white-hot pools of unholy terror—held back from his mind now by the thinnest of brittle crusts. That had been long ago, in Lab-controlled training tests.

He knew better, however, than to try to probe into that sort of phenomenon just now. If he did, the probability was that it would spill full over him at about the moment he was getting his attack under way—which would be, rather definitely, fatal.

But there were other methods of emotional control, simple but generally effective, which might help steady him over the seconds remaining:

There was, for example, the undeniably satisfying reflection that not only had the major disaster of a Ceetal-dominated galaxy been practically averted almost as soon as it was recognized, but that in the same operation—a bonus from Lady Luck!—the long, long hunt for one of civilization's most ruthless enemies was coming to an unexpectedly sudden end. Like the avenging power of Vega personified was the deadly machine behind him, guided by a mind which was both more and less than his own, as it traced its graceful geometrical paths about the doomed yacht. Each completed circle would presently indicate that exactly one more minute had passed of the twenty which were the utmost remaining of U-1's life.

Just as undeniable, of course, was the probability that Pagadan's lease on life would run out even sooner than that—if she still lived.

But there wasn't much he could do about it. If he waited for the Vegan destroyers to arrive, the Lannai would have no chance at all. No normal being could survive another six hours under the kind of deliberately measured mental pressure U-1 would be exerting on her now to drain every possible scrap of information through her disintegrating protective patterns.

By acting as he was, he was giving her the best chance she could get after he had sent her in to spring the trap about U-1 on Gull. In the circumstances, that, too, had been unavoidable. Ironically, the only alternative to killing U-1 outright, as she no doubt had tried to do, was to blunder into one of the situational traps indicated by Correlation, and so restore that grim spacer to his own savage personality—which could then be counted on to cope with any Ceetal attempt to subordinate him once more to their purposes.

Waiting the few hours until he could get there to do the job himself might have made the difference between the survival or collapse of civilization not many decades away. If he had hesitated, the Department would have sent the Interstellar operative in, as a matter of course—officially, and at the risk of compromising the whole Lannai alliance as a consequence.

No, there hadn't been any real choice—the black thoughts rushed on—but just the same it was almost a relief to turn from that fact to the other one that his own chances of survival, just now, were practically as bad. Actually, there was no particular novelty in knowing he was outmatched. Only by being careful to remain the aggressor always, consciously and in fact, by selecting time and place and method of attack, was he able regularly to meet the superiority of the monstrous mentalities that were an Agent's most specific game. And back of him had been always the matchless resources of the Confederacy, to be drawn on as and when he needed them.

Now that familiar situational pattern was almost completely reversed. U-1, doomed himself as surely as human efforts could doom him, had still been able to determine the form of the preliminary attack and force his enemy to adopt it.

So, as usual, the encounter would develop by plan, but the plan would not be Iliff's. His, for once, was to be the other role, that of the blundering, bewildered quarry, tricked into assault, then rushed through it to be struck down at the instant most favorable to the hunter.

Almost frantically, he tore his mind back from the trap. But it was just a little late—the swirling terror had touched him, briefly, and he knew his chances of success were down by that further unnecessary fraction.

Then the two-hundred-foot fire-studded bulk of the yacht came flashing toward him, blotting out space; and as he braked his jets for the approach he had time to remind himself that the quarry's rush did, after all, sometimes carry it through to the hunter. And that, in any event, he'd thought it all out and decided he still disliked an unfinished job— and that he *had* liked Pagadan.

Swinging himself up to the yacht's forward spacelock, every weapon at the ready, he caught the robot's brief thought:

"He's waiting for you! All locks have been released from inside."

Iliff's "Hm-m-m!" was a preoccupied salute to his opponent's logic. The lock had swung gently open before him—there was, of course, no point in attempting to hold it closed against a more powerful ship's sucking tractors; it would, simply, have been destroyed. Gingerly, he floated up to and through the opening, rather like a small balloon of greenish steel-alloy in his bulky armor.

No force-field gripped at his defenses, no devastating bolts of radiant energy crashed at him from the inner walls. That spectral, abnormal terror of a moment ago became a dim sensation which stirred somewhere far down in his mind—and was gone.

He was on the job.

He drove through the inner transmitter, and felt the telepathic barrier that had blanked out the yacht dissolve and reform again behind him. In that instant, he dropped his shields and sent his mind racing full-open through the ship's interior.

There was the briefest of flickering, distorted thought-images from Pagadan. No message, no awareness of his presence—only the unconscious revelation of mind, still alive but strained to the utmost, already marked by the incoherence of ultimate exhaustion. As he sensed it, it vanished. Something had driven smoothly, powerfully, and impenetrably between—something that covered the Lannai's mind like a smothering fog.

Iliff's shields went up just in time. Then he himself was swaying, physically, under as stunning a mental attack as he had ever sustained.

Like the edge of a heavy knife, the impalpable but destructive force sheared at him—slashed once, twice, and was flicked away before he could grip it, leaving his vision momentarily blurred, his nerve-centers writhing.

A wash of corrosive atomic fire splashed blindingly off the front of his armor as he appeared in the control-room door—through it twin narrow-beam tractor rays came ramming in reversed, brain-jarring thrusts at his face-piece. He drove quickly into the room and let the tractors slam him back against the wall. They could not harm him. They were meant to startle and confuse, to destroy calculation before the critical assault.

The fire was different. For perhaps a minute, his armor could continue to absorb it, but no longer. He was being hurried into the attack from every side. There had been no serious attempt to keep him from getting to the control room—he was meant to come to it.

He saw Pagadan first then, as he was meant to see her. Halfway down the narrow room, she sat facing him, only a few feet from the raised control platform against the wall, across which the projector fire came flashing in bluish twelve-inch jets. She was in an ordinary space-suit—no armor. She sat rigid and motionless, blocking his advance down that side of the room because the suit she wore would have burst into incandescence at the first splash of the hellish energies pouring dangerously past her.

U-1 made the point obvious—since he was here to get his ally out of the trap, he could not kill her.

He accepted the logic of that by flicking himself farther along the opposite wall, drawing the fire behind him. As he did so, something like a giant beetle shifted position beyond the massive steel desk on the control platform and dipped from sight again, and he knew then that U-1 was in armor almost as massive as his own—armor that had been a part of Pagadan's Interstellar equipment. To the end, that was the only glimpse he had of the spacer.

There remained then only the obvious frontal attack with mind-shields locked—across the platform to bring his own powerful projectors to bear directly on his opponent's armor.

If he *could* do that, he would very likely win almost instantly, and without injuring Pagadan. Therefore, whatever was to happen to him would happen in the instant of time he was crossing the room to reach the spacer.

And his gamble must be that his armor would carry him through it.

Some eight seconds had passed since he entered the room. A stubby tentacle on the front of his chest armor now raised a shielded projectile gun and sprayed the top of the desk beyond which U-1 crouched with a mushrooming, adhesive blanket of incendiaries. The tractor rays, their controls smothered in that liquid flaring, ceased to be a distraction; and Iliff launched himself.

The furious glare of U-1's projectors winked out abruptly. The force that slammed Iliff down on the surface of the platform was literally bone-shattering.

For an endless, agonizing instant of time he was in the grip of the giant power that seemed to be wrenching him down into the solid hull of the ship. Then, suddenly released, he was off the edge of the platform and on the floor beside it. Momentarily, at least, it took him out of the spacer's line of fire.

But that was about all. He felt bones in his shattered right arm grinding on each other like jagged pebbles as he tried to reach for the studs that would drive him upward again. Throughout his body, torn muscles and crushed nerve-fibers were straining to the dictates of a brain long used to interpret physical pain as a danger signal only; but to activate any of the instruments of the miniature floating tank that incased him was utterly impossible.

He was doubly imprisoned then—in that two and a half ton coffin, and in ruined flesh that jerked aimlessly in animal agonies or had gone flaccid and unfeeling. But his brain, under its multiple separate protective devices, retained partial control; while the mind that was himself was still taut as a coiled snake, bleakly unaffected by the physical disaster.

He knew well enough what had happened. In one titanic jolt, the control platform's gravity field had received the full flow of the projector's energies. It had burned out almost instantaneously under that incalculable overload—but not quite fast enough to save him.

And now U-1's mind came driving in, probing for the extent of his enemy's helplessness, then coldly eager for the kill. At contact range, it would be only a matter of seconds to burn through that massive but no longer dangerous armor and blast out the life that lingered within.

Dimly, Iliff felt him rise and start forward. He felt the probing thoughts flick about him again, cautious still, and

then the mind-shields relaxing and opening out triumphant-
ly as the spacer approached. He dropped his own shields,
and struck.

Never before had he dared risk the sustained concentra-
tion of destructive energy he hurled into U-1's mind—for,
in its way, it was an overload as unstable as that which
had wrecked the gravity field. Instantly, the flaring lights
before his face-piece spun into blackness. The hot taste of
gushing blood in his mouth, the last sensation of straining
lungs and pain-rocked twitching nerves vanished together.
Blocked suddenly and completely from every outward
awareness, he had become a bodiless force bulleting with
deadly resolution upon another.

The attack must have shaken even U-1's battle-hardened
soul to its core. Physically, it stopped in mid-stride, held
him rigid and immobilized with nearly the effect of a paralysis gun. But after the first near-fatal moment of shock,
while he attempted automatically and unsuccessfully to restore his shields before that rush of destruction, he was
fighting back—and not with a similar suicidal fury but with
a grim cold weight of vast mental power which yielded
further ground only slowly if at all.

With that, the struggle became so nearly a stalemate that
it still meant certain victory for the spacer. Both knew the
last trace of physical life would drain out of Iliff in minutes,
though perhaps only Iliff realized that his mind must destroy
itself even more swiftly.

Something tore through his consciousness then like jagged
bolts of lightning. He thought it was death. But it came
again and again—until a slow, tremendous surprise welled
up in him:

It was the *other* mind which was being torn! Dissolving
now, crumbling into flashing thought-convulsions like tor-
tured shrieks, though it still struggled on against him—and
against something else, something which was by then completely beyond Iliff's comprehension.

The surprise dimmed out, together with his last awareness of himself—still driving relentlessly in upon a hated
foe who would not die.

The voice paused briefly, then added: "Get that part to Lab. They'll be happy to know they hit it pretty close, for once."

It stopped again. After a moment the bright-looking young man in the Jeltad Headquarters office inquired, not too deferentially:

"Is there anything else, sir?"

He'd glanced up curiously once or twice at the vision tank of the extreme-range communicator before him, while he deftly distributed Iliff's after-mission report through the multiple-recorders. However, it wasn't the first time he'd seen a Zone Agent check in from the Emergency Treatment Chamber of his ship, completely inclosed in a block of semisolid protective gel, through which he was being molded, rayed, dosed, drenched, shocked, nourished and psychoed back to health and sanity.

With the irreverence of youth, the headquarters man considered that these near-legendary heroes of the Department bore on such occasions, when their robots even took care of heartbeat and breathing for them, a striking resemblance to damaged and bad-tempered embryos. He hoped suddenly no one happened to be reading his mind.

"Connect me," Iliff's voice said, though the lips of the figure in the vision tank did not move, "with Three for a personal report."

"I've been listening," came the deep modulated reply from an invisible source. "Switch off, Lallebeth—you've got all you need. All clear now, Iliff—and once more, congratulations!" And the picture of the tall, gray-haired, lean-faced man, who was the Third Co-ordinator of the Vegan Confederacy, grew slowly through the telepath transmitter into the mind of the small, wiry shape—half restored and covered with irregular patches of new pink skin—in the ship's Emergency Treatment Chamber.

"Back in the tank again, eh?" the Co-ordinator observed critically. "For the second day after a mission, you don't look too bad." He paused, considering Iliff closely. "Gravity?" he inquired.

"Gravity!" admitted the embryo.

"That will mess a fellow up!" The Co-ordinator was nod-

ding sympathetically, but it seemed to Iliff that his superior's mind was on other matters, and more pleasing
ones.

"Lab's just going to have to design me a suit," Three
ran on with his usual chattiness, "which will be nonreactive
to any type of synthetigravs, including tractors. Theoretically impossible, they say, of course! But I'm sure the right
approach—"

He interrupted himself:

"I imagine you'll want to know what happened after she
got you back to your ship and contacted the destroyers?"

"She left word she was going to get in touch with you
on her way back to Jeltad," Iliff said.

"Well, she did that. A remarkably energetic sort of person in a quiet way, Iliff. Fully aware, too, as I discovered,
of the political possibilities in the situation. I persuaded her,
of course, to take official credit for the death of U-1,
and the termination of that part of the Ceetal menace—
and, incidentally, for saving the life of one of our Department Agents."

"That wasn't so incidental," Iliff remarked.

"Only in comparison with the other, of course. She really
did it then?"

"Oh, she did it all right! I was on my way out fast
when she turned him down. Must have been a bad shock
to U-1. I understand he hadn't released her mind for more
than three or four seconds before she was reaching for his
projector."

The Co-ordinator nodded. "The mental resiliency of these
highly developed telepathic races must be really extraordinary! Any human being would have remained paralyzed
for minutes after such pressures—perhaps for hours. Well, he
wasn't omniscient, after all. He thought he could just let
her lie there until he was finished with you."

"How long had he been pouring it on her?"

"About four hours! Practically ever since they hit space,
coming out from Gull."

"She didn't crack at all?" Iliff asked curiously.

"No, but she thinks she couldn't have lasted more than
another hour. However, she seemed to have had no doubt

that *you* would arrive and get her out of the mess in time. Rather flattering, eh?"

The agent considered. "No," he said then. "Not necessarily."

His superior chuckled. "At any rate, she was reluctant to take credit for U-1. She thought if she accepted, you might feel she didn't fully appreciate your plunging in to the rescue."

"Well, you seem to have reassured her. And now, just what are the political results going to be?"

"It's too early to say definitely, but even without any help from us they'd be pretty satisfactory. The Ceetal business isn't for public consumption, of course—the boys made a clean sweep of that bunch a few hours back, by the way—but there've always been plenty of idiots building U-1 up into a glamorous figure. The Mysterious Great Bandit of the Spaceways and that sickening kind of stuff. They'll whoop it up just as happily now for the Champion of Vegan Justice who sent the old monster on his way, to wit—the Lannai Pagadan! It won't hurt either that she's really beautiful.

"And through her, of course, the glamor reflects back on her people, our nonhuman allies."

Iliff said thoughtfully: "Think they'll stay fashionable long enough to cinch the alliance?"

The Co-ordinator looked rather smug. "I believe that part of it can be safely left to me! Especially," he added deliberately, "since most of the organized resistance to said alliance has already collapsed."

Iliff waited and made no comment, because when the old boy got as confidential as all that, he was certainly leading up to something. And he did not usually bother to lead up to things without some good reason—which almost always spelled a lot of trouble for somebody else.

There was nobody else around at all, except Iliff.

"I had an unexpected visit three days ago," the Co-ordinator continued, "from my colleague, the Sixteenth Co-ordinator, Department of Cultures. He'd been conducting, he said, a personal investigation of Lannai culture and psychology—and had found himself forced to the conclusion there was no reasonable objection to having them join us as full members of the Confederacy. 'A people of extraordinary refinement . . . high moral standards—' Hinted we'd have no further trouble with the Traditionalists either. Remarkable change of heart, eh?"

"Remarkable!" Iliff agreed, watchfully.

"But can you imagine," inquired the Co-ordinator, "what brought Sixteen—between us, mind you, Iliff, as pig-headed and hidebound an obstructionist as the Council has been hampered by in centuries—to this state of uncharacteristic enlightenment?"

"No," Iliff said, "I can't."

"Wait till you hear this then! After we'd congratulated each other and so on, he brought the subject back to various Lannai with whom he'd become acquainted. It developed presently he was interested in the whereabouts of one particular Lannai he'd met in a social way right here on Jeltad a few weeks before. He understood she was doing work—"

"All right," Iliff interrupted. "It was Pagadan."

The Co-ordinator appeared disappointed. "Yes, it was. She told you she'd met him, did she?"

"She admitted to some circulating in our upper social levels," Iliff said. "What did you tell him?"

"That she was engaged in highly confidential work for the Department at present, but that we expected to hear from her within a few days—I had my fingers crossed there!—and that I'd see to it she heard he'd been inquiring about her. Afterwards, after he'd gone, I sat down and sweated blood until I got her message from the destroyer."

"You don't suspect, I suppose, that she might have psychoed him?"

"Nonsense, Iliff!" the Co-ordinator smiled blandly. "If I had the *slightest* suspicion of that, it would be my duty to investigate immediately. Wouldn't it? But now, there's one point—your robot, of course, made every effort to keep Pagadan from realizing there was no human crew manning the ship. However, she told me frankly she'd caught on to our little Department secret and suggested that the best way to keep it there would be to have her transferred from Interstellar to Galactic. As a manner of fact, she's requested Zone Agent training! Think she'd qualify?"

"Oh, she'll qualify!" Iliff said dryly. "At that, it might be a good idea to get her into the Department, where we can try to keep an eye on her. It would be too bad if we found out, ten years from now, that a few million Lannai were running the Confederacy."

For an instant, the Co-ordinator looked startled. "Hm-m-m," he said reflectively. "Well, that's hardly likely. However, I think I'll take your advice. I might send her over to your Zone in a week or so, and——"

"Oh, no," Iliff said quietly. "Oh, no, you don't! I've been waiting right along for the catch, and this is one job Headquarters is going to swing without me."

"No, Iliff——"

"It's never happened before," Iliff added, "but right now the Department is very close to its first case of Zone Agent mutiny."

"Now, Iliff, take it easy!" The Co-ordinator paused. "I must disapprove of your attitude, of course, but frankly I admire your common sense. Well, forget the suggestion—I'll find some other sucker."

He became pleasantly official.

"I suppose you're on your way back to your Zone at present?"

"I am. In fact, we're almost exactly in the position we'd reached when you buzzed me the last time. Now, there wouldn't happen to be some little job I could knock off for you on the way?"

"Well——" the Co-ordinator began, off guard. For the shortest fraction of a second, he had the air of a man consulting an over-stuffed mental file.

Then he started and blinked.

"In your condition? Nonsense, Iliff! It's out of the question!"

On the last word, Iliff's thought and image flickered out of his mind. But the Third Co-ordinator sat motionless for another moment or so before he turned off the telepath transmitter. There was a look of mild surprise on his face.

Of course, there had been no change of expression possible in that immobilized and anaesthetized embryonic figure— not so much as the twitch of an eyelid! But in that instant, while he was hesitating, there *had* seemed to flash from it a blast of such cold and ferocious malignity that he was almost startled into flipping up his shields.

"Better lay off the little devil for a while!" he decided. "Let him just stick to his routine. I'll swear, for a moment there I saw smoke pour out of his ears."

He reached out and tapped a switch.

"Psych-tester? What do you think?"

"The Agent requires no deconditioning," the Psych-tester's mechanical voice stated promptly. "As I predicted at the time, his decision to board U-1's ship was in itself sufficient to dissolve both the original failure-shock and the artificial conditioning later connected with it. The difficulties he experienced, between the decision and his actual entry of the ship, were merely symptoms of that process and have had no further effect on his mental health."

The Co-ordinator rubbed his chin reflectively.

"Well, that sounds all right. Does he realize I . . . uh . . . had anything to do—?"

"The Agent is strongly of the opinion that you suspected Tahmey of being U-1 when you were first informed of the Interstellar operative's unusual report, and further, that you assigned him to the mission for this reason. While approving of the choice as such, he shows traces of a sub-level reflection that your tendency towards secretiveness will lead you to . . . outfox . . . yourself so badly some day that he may not be able to help you."

"Why—"

"He has also begun to suspect," the Psych-tester continued, undisturbed, "that he was fear-conditioned over a period of years to the effect that any crisis involving U-1 would automatically create the highest degree of defensive tensions compatible with his type of mentality."

The Co-ordinator whistled softly.

"He's caught on to that, eh?" He reflected. "Well, after all," he pointed out, almost apologetically, "it wasn't such a bad idea in itself! The boy does have this tendency to bull his way through, on some short-cut or other, to a rather dangerous degree. And there was no way of foreseeing the complications introduced by the Ceetal threat and his sense of responsibility towards the Lannai, which made it impossible for him to obey that urgent mental pressure to be careful in whatever he did about U-1."

He paused invitingly, but the Psych-tester made no comment.

"It's hard to guess right every time!" the Co-ordinator concluded defensively.

He shook his head and sighed, but then forgot Iliff entirely as he turned to the next problem.

THE ILLUSIONISTS

THE THREE Bjanta scouts were within an hour's flight of the yellow dwarf star of Ulphi where the *Viper's* needle-shape drove into their detection range, high up but on a course that promised almost to intersect their own.

It didn't exactly come to that point, though the unwary newcomer continued to approach for several minutes more. But then, with an abruptness which implied considerable shock on board at discovering Bjanta ahead, she veered off sharply and shot away at a very respectable speed.

The scout disks swung about unhurriedly, opened out in pursuit formation and were presently closing in again, with leisurely caution, on the fugitive. Everything about that beautifully designed, blue-gleaming yacht suggested the most valuable sort of catch. Some very wealthy individual's plaything it might have been, out of one of the major centers of civilization, though adventuring now far from the beaten path of commercial spaceways. In which case, she would be very competently piloted and crewed and somewhat better armed than the average freighter. Which should make her capable of resisting their combined attack for a maximum of four or five minutes—or, if she preferred energy-devouring top velocity, of keeping ahead of them for even one or two minutes longer than that.

But no Bjanta was ever found guilty of impulsive reck-
lessness. And, just possibly, this yacht could also turn out
to be another variation of those hellish engines of destruction which Galactic humanity and its allies had been developing with ever-increasing skill during the past few thousand years, against just such marauders as they.

As it happened, that described the *Viper* exactly. A Vegan
G.Z. Agent-Ship, and one of the last fifty or so of her
type to be completed, she was, compared with anything
else up to five times her three-hundred-foot length, the
peak, the top, the absolute culmination of space-splitting
sudden death. And, furthermore, she knew it.

"They're maintaining pattern and keeping up with no
sign of effort," her electronic brain reported to her pilot.
"Should we show them a little more speed?"

"The fifteen percent increase was plenty," the pilot returned in a pleasant soprano voice. Her eyes, the elongated
silver eyes and squared black pupils of a Lannai humanoid,
studied the Bjantas' positions in the vision tank of the long,
wide control desk at which she sat. "If they edge in too
far, you can start weaving, but remember they're sensiitve
little apes! Anything fancy before we get within range of
our cruiser is bound to scare them off."

There was silence for a moment. Then the ship's robot
voice came into the control room again.

"Pagadan, the disk low in Sector Twelve is almost at contact beaming range. We could take any two of them at
any moment now, and save the third for the test run!"

"I know it, little *Viper*," Pagadan said patiently. "But this
whole job's based on the assumption that the Bjantas
are operating true to form. In that case, the Mother Disk
should be somewhere within three light-years behind us, and
the cruiser wants to run two of these scouts back far enough
to show just where it's lying. We need only the one for ourselves."

Which was something the *Viper* already knew. But it
had been designed to be a hunting machine more nearly
than anything else, and at times its hunting impulses had to
be diverted. Pagadan did that as automatically as she would
have checked a similar impulse in her own mind—in effect,

whenever she was on board, there was actually no very definite boundary between her own thoughts and those that pulsed through the *Viper*. Often the Lannai would have found it difficult to say immediately whether it was her organic brain or its various electronic extensions in the ship which was attending to some specific bit of business. Just now, as an example, it was the *Viper* who had been watching the communicators.

"The Agent-Trainee on the O-Ship off Ulphi is trying to talk to you, Pagadan," the robot-voice came into the room. "Will you adjust to his range?"

The Lannai's silver-nailed hand shot out and spun a tiny dial on the desk before her. From a communicator to her left a deep voice inquired, a little anxiously:

"Pag? Do you hear me? This is Hallerock, Pag?"

"Go ahead, chum!" she invited. "I was off beam for a moment there. The planet still look all right?"

"No worse than it ever did," said Hallerock. "But this is about your Fleet operation. The six destroyers are spread out behind you in interception positions by now, and the cruiser should be coming into detection dead ahead at any moment. You still want them to communicate with you through the Observation Ship here?"

"Better keep it that way," Pagadan ordered. "The Bjantas might spot Fleet signals, as close to me as they are, but it's a cinch they can't tap *this* beam! I won't slip up again. Anything from the Department?"

"Correlation is sending some new stuff out on the Ulphi business, but nothing important. At any rate, they didn't want to break into your maneuver with the Bjantas. I told them to home it here to the O-Ship. Right?"

"Right," Pagadan approved. "You'll make a Zone Agent yet, my friend! In time."

"I doubt it," Hallerock grunted. "There's no real future in it anyway. Here's the cruiser calling again, Pag! I'll be standing by—"

Pagadan pursed her lips thoughtfully as a barely audible click indicated her aide had gone off communication. She'd been a full-fledged Zone Agent of the Vegan Confederacy for exactly four months now—the first member of any nonhuman race to attain that rank in the super-secretive Department of Galactic Zones. Hallerock, human, was an advanced Trainee. Just how advanced was a question she'd have to decide, and very soon.

The surface reflections vanished from her mind at the *Viper's* sub-vocal warning:

"Cruiser—dead ahead!"

"The disk on your left!" Pagadan snapped. "Cut it off from the others as soon as they begin to turn. Give it a *good* start then—and be sure you're crowding the last bit of speed out of it before you even think of closing in. We may not be able to get what we're after—probably won't —but Lab can use every scrap of information we collect on those babies!"

"We'll get what we're after, too," the *Viper* almost purred. And, a bare instant later:

"They've spotted the cruiser. *Now!*"

In the vision tank, the fleeing disk grew and grew. During the first few minutes, it had appeared there only as a comet-tailed spark, a dozen radiant streamers of different colors fanning out behind it—not an image of the disk itself but the tank's visual representation of any remote moving object on which the ship's detectors were held. The shifting lengths and brightness of the streamers announced at a glance to those trained to read them the object's distance, direction, comparative and absolute speeds and other matters of interest to a curious observer.

But as the *Viper* began to reduce the headstart the Bjanta had been permitted to get, at the exact rate calculated to incite it to the most intensive efforts to hold that lead, a shadowy outline of the disk's true shape began to grow about the spark. A bare quarter million miles away finally, the disk itself appeared to be moving at a visual range of two hundred yards ahead of the ship, while the spark still flickered its varied information from the center of the image.

Pagadan's hands, meanwhile, played continuously over the control desk's panels, racing the ship's recording instruments through every sequence of descriptive analysis of which they were capable.

"We're still getting nothing really new, I'm afraid," she said at last, matter-of-factly. She had never been within sight of a Bjanta before; but Vega's Department of Galactic Zones had copies of every available record ever made of them, and she had studied the records. The information was largely repetitious and not conclusive enough to have ever permitted a really decisive thrust against the marauders. Bjantas no longer constituted a major threat to civilization, but they had never stopped being a dangerous nuisance along its fringes—space-vermin of a particularly elusive and obnoxious sort.

"They've made no attempt to change direction at all?" she inquired.

"Not since they first broke out of their escape-curve," the *Viper* replied. "Shall I close in now?"

"Might as well, I suppose." Pagadan was still gazing, almost wistfully, into the tank. The disk was tilted slightly sideways, dipping and quivering in the familiar motion-pattern of Bjanta vessels; a faint glimmer of radiation ran and vanished and ran again continuously around its yard-thick edge. The Bjantas were conservatives; the first known recordings made of them in the early centuries of the First Empire had shown space-machines of virtually the same appearance as the one now racing ahead of the *Viper*.

"The cruiser seems satisfied we check with its own line on the Mother Disk," she went on. She sighed, tapping the tank anxiously. "Well, nudge them a bit—and be ready to jump!"

The *Viper's* nudging was on the emphatic side. A greenish, transparent halo appeared instantly about the disk; a rainbow-hued one flashed into visibility just beyond it immediately after. Then the disk's dual barrier vanished again; and the disk itself veered crazily off its course, flipping over and over like a crippled bat, showing at every turn the deep, white-hot gash the *Viper's* touch and seared across its top.

It was on the fifth turn, some four-tenths of a second later, that it split halfway around its rim. Out of that yawning mouth a few score minute duplicates of itself were spewed into space and flashed away in all directions—individual Bjantas in their equivalent of a combined spacesuit and lifeboat. As they dispersed the stricken scout gaped wider; a blinding glare burst out of it; and the disk had vanished in the traditional Bjanta style of self-destruction when trapped by superior force.

Fast as the reaction had been, the *Viper's* forward surge at full accceleration following her first jabbing beam was barely slower. She stopped close enough to the explosion to feel its radiations activate her own barriers; and even before she stopped, every one of her grappling devices was fully extended and combing space about her.

Within another two seconds, therefore, each of the fleeing Bjantas was caught—and at the instant of contact, all but two had followed the scout into explosive and practically traceless suicide. Those two, however, were wrenched open by paired tractors which gripped and simultaneously twisted as they gripped—an innovation with which the *Viper* had been outfitted for this specific job.

Pagadan, taut and watching, went white and was on her feet with a shriek of inarticulate triumph.

"You *did* it, you sweetheart!" she yelped then. "First ones picked up intact in five hundred years!"

"They're not intact," the *Viper* corrected, less excitedly. "But I have all the pieces, I think!"

"The bodies are hardly damaged," gloated Pagadan, staring into the tank. "It doesn't matter much about the shells. Just bring it all in easy now! The lovely things! Wait till Lab hears we got them."

She hovered around nervously while the flat, brown, soft-shelled—and really not badly dented—bodies of the two Bjantas were being drawn in through one of the *Viper's* locks and deposited gently in a preservative tank, where they floated against the top, their twenty-two angular legs folded up tightly against their undersides. Most of the bunched neural extensions that made them a unit with the mechanisms of their detachable space-shells had been sheared off, of course; but the *Viper had* saved everything.

"Nice work, Pag!" Hallerock's voice came from the communicator as she returned exultantly to the control room. "No chance of any life being left in those things, I suppose?"

"Not after that treatment!" Pagadan said regretfully. "But I'm really not complaining. You heard me then?"

"I did," acknowledged Hallerock. "Paralyzing sort of war whoop you've got! Want to see the recording the cruiser shot back to me on the Mother Disk? That run just went off, too, as per schedule."

"Put it on!" Pagadan said, curling herself comfortably and happily into her desk chair. "So they found Mommy, eh? Never had such fun before I started slumming around with humans. What were the destructive results?"

"They did all right. An estimated forty-five percent of the scouts right on the strike—and they figure it will be over eighty before the survivors get out of pursuit range. One of the destroyers and a couple of the cruiser's strikeships were slightly damaged when the core blew up. Nothing serious."

The visual recording appeared on the communication screen a moment later. It was very brief, as seen from the cruiser—following its hornet-swarm of released strikeships in on the great, flat, scaly-looking pancake bulk of the Mother Disk, while a trio of destroyers closed down on either side. As a fight, Pagadan decided critically, it was also the worst flop she'd seen in years, considering that the trapped quarry was actually a layered composite of several thousand well-armed scouts! For a brief instant, the barriers of every charging Vegan ship blazed a warning white; then the screen filled momentarily with a rainbow-hued sparkle of scouts scattering under the lethal fire of the attackers— and the brighter flashing of those that failed.

As both darkened out and the hunters swirled off in pursuit of the fugitive swarms, an ellipsoid crystalline core, several hundred yards in diameter, appeared where the Disk had lain in space. The Bjanta breeding center—

It seemed to expand slightly.

An instant later, it was a miniature nova.

Pagadan blinked and nodded approvingly as the screen went blank.

"Tidy habit! Saves us a lot of trouble. But *we* made the only real haul of the day, *Viper,* old girl!" She grimaced. "So now we've still got to worry about that sleepwalking silly little planet of Ulphi, and the one guy on it who isn't . . . isn't sleepwalking, anyway. And a couple of other—" She straightened up suddenly. "Who's that working your communicators now?"

"That's the robot-tracker you put on the Department of Cultures investigator on Ulphi," the *Viper* informed her. "He wants to come in to tell you the lady's got herself into some kind of jam with the population down there. Shall I switch him to the O-Ship and have the Agent-Trainee check and take over, if necessary?"

"Hold it!" Pagadan's hands flew out towards the section of instrument panel controlling the communicators. "Not if it's the D. C. girl! That would mess up all my plans. The tracker's ready and equipped to see nothing happens to her before I get there. Just put that line through to me, fast!"

Some while later, she summoned Hallerock to the O-Ship's communicator.

". . . So I'm picking you up in a few minutes and taking you on board the *Viper.* Central Lab wants a set of structural recordings of these pickled Bjantas right away— and you'll have to do it, because I won't have the time."

"What happened?" her aide inquired, startled.

"Nothing very serious," Pagadan said soothingly. "But it's likely to keep me busy for the next few hours. Our D. C. investigator on Ulphi may have got an accidental whiff of what's rancid on the planet—anyway, somebody's trying to get her under mental control right now! I've got her covered by a tracker, of course, so she's in no real danger; but I'll take the *Viper's* skiff and go on down as soon as I get you on board. By the way, how soon can you have the hospital ship prepared for its job?"

Hallerock hesitated a moment. "I suppose it's ready to start any time. I finished treating the last of the personnel four hours ago."

"Good boy," Pagadan applauded. "I've got something in mind—not sure yet whether it will work. But that attack on the D. C. might make it possible for us to wind up the whole Ulphi operation inside the next twenty-four hours!"

It had started out, three weeks before, looking like such a nice little mission. Since it was her fifth assignment in four months, and since there had been nothing even remotely nice about any of the others, Pagadan could appreciate that.

Nothing much to do for about three or four weeks now, she'd thought gratefully as she hauled out her skiff for a brief first survey of the planet of Ulphi. She had landed as an ostensible passenger on a Vegan destroyer, the skiff tucked away in one of the destroyer's gun locks, while the *Viper* went on orbit at a safe distance overhead. That gleaming deep-space machine looked a trifle too impressive to be a suitable vehicle for Pelial, the minor official of Galactic Zones, which was Pagadan's local alias. And as Ulphi's entire population was planet-bound by congenital space-fear, the skiff would provide any required amount of transportation, while serving principally as living quarters and a work-office.

But there would be really nothing to do. Except, of course, to keep a casual eye on the safety of the other Vegans newly arrived on the planet and co-operate with the Fleet in its unhurried preparations to receive the Bjantas, who were due to appear in about a month for the ninth of their series of raids on Ulphi. Those obliging creatures conducted their operations in cycles of such unvarying regularity that it was a pleasure to go to work on them, once you'd detected their traces and could muster superior force to intercept their next return.

On Ulphi Bjantas had been reaping their harvest of life and what they could use of civilization's treasures and tools at periods which lay just a fraction over three standard years apart. It had done no very significant damage as yet, since it had taken eight such raids to frighten the population into revealing its plight by applying for membership in the far-off Confederacy of Vega and the protection that would bring them. The same cosmic clockwork which first set the great Disk on this course would be returning it now, predictably, to the trap Vega had prepared.

Nothing for Pagadan to worry about. Nobody, actually, seemed to have much confidence that the new shell-cracker beams installed on the *Viper* to pick up a couple of Bjantas in an unexploded condition would work as they should, but that problem was Lab's and not hers. And, feeling no doubt that she'd earned a little vacation, they were presenting her meanwhile with these next three weeks on Ulphi. The reports of the officials of other Confederacy government branches who had preceded Pagadan here had described it as a uniquely charming little backwater world of humanity, cut off by the development of planetary space-fear from the major streams of civilization for nearly four hundred years. Left to itself in its amiable climate, Ulphi had flowered gradually into a state of quaint and leisurely prettiness.

So went the reports!

Jauntily, then, Pagadan set forth in her skiff to make an aerial survey of this miniature jewel of civilization and pick out a few of the very best spots for some solid, drowsy loafing.

Two days later, her silver hair curled flat to her skull with outraged shock, she came back on board the *Viper*. The activated telepath transmitter hummed with the ship's full power, as it hurled her wrathful message to G. Z. Headquarters Central on the planet of Jeltad—in Vega's system, eight thousand light-years away.

At Central on Jeltad, a headquarters clerk, on his way out to lunch, paused presently behind the desk of another. His manner was nervous.

"What's the Pyramid Effect?" he inquired.

"You ought to know," his friend replied. "If you don't, go punch it from Restricted Psych-Library under that heading. I've got a final mission report coming through." He glanced around. "How come the sudden urge for knowledge, Linky?"

Linky jerked a thumb back towards his desk transmitter. "I got that new Lannai Z. A. on just before the end of my stretch. She was blowing her silver top about things in general—had me lining up interviews with everybody from Snoops to the Old Man for her! The Pyramid Effect seems to be part of it."

The other clerk snickered. "She's just diving into a mission then. I had her on a few times while she was in Zonal Training. She'll swear like a Terran till she hits her stride. After that, the rougher things get the sweeter she grows. You want to wait a little? If I get this beam through, I'll turn it over to a recorder and join you for lunch."

"All right." Linky hesitated a moment and then drifted back towards his desk. At a point well outside the vision range of its transmitter screen, he stopped and listened.

". . . Well, *why* didn't anybody know?" Pagadan's voice came, muted but crackling. "That Department of Cultures investigator has been on Ulphi for over a month now, and others just as long! You get copies of their reports, don't you? You couldn't put any two of them together without seeing that another Telep-Two thinks he's invented the Pyramid Effect out here—there isn't a thing on the crummy little planet that doesn't show it! And I'll be the daughter of a C-Class human," she added bitterly, "if it isn't a type-case in full flower, with all the trimmings! Including immortalization and the Siva Psychosis. No, I do *not* want Lab to home any of their findings out to me! Tell them I'm staying right here on telepath till they've sorted out what I gave them. Where's Snoops, that evil little man? Or can somebody locate that fuddle-headed, skinny, blond clerk I had on a few minutes—"

Linky tiptoed gently back out of hearing.

"She's talking to Correlation now," he reported to his friend. "Not at the sweetness stage yet. I think I'll put in a little time checking the Library at that."

The other clerk nodded without looking up. "You could use the Head's information cabinet. He just went out."

"Pyramid Effect," Psych-Library Information instructed Linky gently a minute later. "Restricted, Galactic Zones. Result of the use of an expanding series of psychimpulsemultipliers, organic or otherwise, by Telepaths of the Orders Two to Four, for the transference of directional patterns, compulsions, illusions, et cetera, to large numbers of subjects.

"The significant feature of the Pyramid Effect is its elimination of excessive drain on the directing mentality, achieved by utilizing the neural or neural-type energies of the multipliers themselves in transferring the directed impulses from one stage to the next.

"Techniques required to establish the first and second stages of multipliers are classified as Undesirable General Knowledge. Though not infrequently developed independently by Telepaths about the primary level, their employment in any form is prohibited throughout the Confederacy of Vega and variously discouraged by responsible governments elsewhere.

"Establishment of the third stage, and subsequent stages, of impulse-multipliers involves a technique-variant rarely developed by uninstructed Telepaths below the Order of Five. It is classified, under all circumstances, as Prohibited General Knowledge and is subject to deletion under the regulations pertaining to that classification.

"Methodology of the Pyramid Effect may be obtained in detail under the heading 'Techniques: Pyramid Effect'—"

The gentle voice subsided.

"H'm-m-m!" said Linky. He glanced about but there was nobody else in immediate range of the information cabinet. He tapped out "Techniques: Pyramid Effect," and punched.

"The information applied for," another voice stated tonelessly, "is restricted to Zone Agent levels and above. Your identification?"

Linky scowled, punched "Cancellation" quickly, murmured "Nuts!" and tapped another set of keys.

"Psychimpulse-multiplier," the gentle voice came back. "Restricted, Galactic Zones. Any person, organic entity, energy form, or mentalized instrument employed in distributing the various types of telepathic impulses to subjects beyond the scope of the directing mentality in range of number— Refer to 'Pyramid Effect'—"

That seemed to be that. What else was the Z. A. crying about? Oh, yes!

"Siva Psychosis," the gentle voice resumed obligingly. "Symptom of the intermediate to concluding stages of the Autocrat Circuit in human-type mentalities— Refer to 'Multiple Murder: Causes'—"

Linky grimaced.

"Got what you wanted?" The other clerk was standing behind him.

Linky got up. "No," he said. "Let's go anyhow. Your Final Mission came through?"

His friend shook his head.

"The guy got it. Ship and all. The automatic death signals just started coming in. That *bong-bong . . . bong-bong* stuff always gets on my nerves!" He motioned Linky into an elevator ahead of him. "They ought to work out a different sort of signal."

"Understand you've been having some trouble with Department of Cultures personnel," Snoops told the transmitter genially.

"Just one of them," Pagadan replied, regarding him with disfavor. Probably, he wasn't really evil but he certainly looked it—aged in evil, and wizened with it. Also, he had been, just now, very hard to find. "That particular one," she added, "is worse than any dozen others I've run into, so far!"

"DC-CFI 1227, eh?" Snoops nodded. "Don't have to make up a dossier for you on her. Got it all ready."

"We've had trouble with her before, then?"

"Oh, sure! Lots of times. System Chief Jasse—beautiful big thing, isn't she?" Snoops chuckled. "I've got any number of three-dimensionals of her."

"You would have," said Pagadan sourly. "For a flagpole, she's not so bad looking, at that. Must be eight feet if she's an inch!"

"Eight foot two," Snoops corrected. "What's she up to now, that place you're at—Ulphi?"

"Minding other people's business like any D. C. Mostly mine, though she doesn't know that. I'm objecting particularly to her practice of pestering the Fleet for information they either don't have or aren't allowed to give for reasons of plain standard operational security. There's a destroyer commander stationed here who says every time she looks at him now, he gets a feeling he'd better watch his step or he'll get turned over and whacked."

"She wouldn't do that," Snoops said earnestly. "She's a good girl, that Jasse. Terribly conscientious, that's all. You want that dossier homed out to you or right now, vocally?"

"Both. Right now I want mostly background stuff, so I'll know how to work her. I'd psycho it out of her myself, but she's using a pretty good mind-shield and I can't spend too much mission-time on the Department of Cultures."

Snoops nodded, cleared his throat, rolled his eyes up reflectively, closed them and began.

Age twenty-five, or near enough to make no difference. Type A-Class Human, unknown racial variant. Citizen of the Confederacy; home-planet Jeltad. Birthplace unknown—parentage, ditto; presumably spacer stock.

"Details on that!" interrupted Pagadan.

He'd intended to, Snoops said, looking patient.

Subject, at about the age of three, had been picked up in space, literally, and in a rather improbable section—high in the northern latitudes where the suns thinned out into the figurative Rim. A Vegan scout, pausing to inspect an area littered with the battle-torn wreckage of four ships, found her drifting about there unconscious and half-alive, in a spacesuit designed for a very tall adult—the kind of adult she eventually became.

Investigation indicated she was the only survivor of what must have been an almost insanely savage and probably very brief engagement. There was some messy evidence that one of the ships had been crewed by either five or six of her kind. The other three had been manned by Lartessians, a branch of human space marauders with whom Vega's patrol forces were more familiar than they particularly wanted to be.

So was Pagadan. "They fight just like that, the crazy apes! And they're no slouches—our little pet's people must be a rugged lot to break even with them at three-to-one odds. But we've got no record at all of that breed?"

He'd checked pretty closely but without results, Snoops shrugged. And so, naturally enough, had Jasse herself later on. She'd grown up in the family of the scout's second pilot. They were earnest Traditionalists, so it wasn't surprising that at sixteen she entered the Traditionalist College on Jeltad. She was a brilliant student and a spectacular athlete—twice a winner in Vega's System Games.

"Doing what?" inquired Pagadan curiously.

Javelin, and one of those swimming events; Snoops wasn't sure just which— She still attended the College intermittently; but at nineteen she'd started to work as a field investigator for the Department of Cultures. Which wasn't surprising either, since Cultures was practically the political extension of the powerful Traditionalist Creed—

They had made her a System Chief only three years later.

"About that time," Snoops concluded, "was when we started having trouble with Jasse. She's smart enough to suspect that whatever Galactic Zones is doing doesn't jibe entirely with our official purpose in life." He looked mildly amused. "Seems to think we might be some kind of secret police—you know how Traditionalists feel about anything like *that!*"

Pagadan nodded. "Everything open and aboveboard. They mean well, bless them!"

She went silent then, reflecting; while the alien black-and-silver eyes continued to look at Snoops, or through him possibly, at something else.

He heard himself saying uneasily, "You're not going to do her any harm, Zone Agent?"

"Now why should I be doing System Chief Jasse any harm?" Pagadan inquired, much too innocently. "A good girl, like you say. And so lovely looking, too—in spite of that eight-foot altitude."

"Eight foot two," Snoops corrected mechanically. He didn't feel at all reassured.

The assistant to the Chief of G.Z. Office of Correlation entered the room to which his superior had summoned him and found the general gazing pensively upon a freshly assembled illumined case-chart.

The assistant glanced at the chart number and shrugged sympathetically.

"I understand she wants to speak to you personally," he remarked. "Is it as bad as she indicates?"

"Colonel Deibos," the general said, without turning his head, "I'm glad you're here. Yes, it's just about as bad!" He nodded at the upper right region of the chart where a massed group of symbols flickered uncertainly. "That's the bulk of the information we got from the Zone Agent concerning the planet of Ulphi just now. Most of the rest of it has been available to this office for weeks."

Both men studied the chart silently for a moment.

"It's a mess, certainly," the colonel admitted then. "But I'm sure the Agent understands that, when an emergency is not indicated in advance, all incoming information is necessarily handled here in a routine manner, which frequently involves a considerable time-lag in correlation."

"No doubt she does," agreed the general. "However, we keep running into her socially when she's around the System, my wife and I. Particularly my wife. You understand that I should like our summation of this case to be as nearly perfect as we can make it?"

"I understand, sir."

"I'm going to read it," the general sighed. "I want you to check me closely. If you're doubtful on any point of interpretation at all, kindly interrupt me at once."

They bent over the chart together.

"The over-all pattern on Ulphi," the general stated, "is obviously that produced by an immortalized A-Class human intellect, Sub-Class Twelve, variant Telep-Two—as developed in planetary or small-system isolation, over a period of between three and five centuries."

He'd lapsed promptly, Colonel Deibos noted with a trace of amusement, into a lecturer's tone and style. Being one of the two men primarily responsible for devising the psychomathematics of correlation and making it understandable to others, the general had found plenty of opportunity to acquire such mannerisms.

"In that time," he went on, "the system of general controls has, of course, become almost completely automatic. There is, however, continuing and fairly intensive activity on the part of the directing mentality. Development of the Siva Psychosis is at a phase typical for the elapsed period—concealed and formalized killings cloaked in sacrificial symbolism. Quantitatively, they have not begun as yet to affect the population level. The open and indiscriminate slaughter preceding the sudden final decline presumably would not appear, then, for at least another century.

"Of primary significance for the identification of the controlling mentality is this central grouping of formulae. Within the historical period which must have seen the early stages of the mentality's dominance, the science of Ulphi—then practically at Galactic par—was channeled for thirty-eight years into a research connected with the various problems of personal organic immortality. Obviously, under such conditions, only the wildest sort of bad luck could prevent discovery and co-ordination of the three basic requirements for any of the forms of individual perpetuation presently developed.

"We note, however, that within the next two years the investigation became completely discredited, was dropped and has not been resumed since.

"The critical date, finally, corresponds roughly to the announced death of the planet's outstanding psychic leader of the time—an historical figure even on present-day Ulphi, known as Moyuscane the Immortal Illusionist.

"Corroborative evidence—"

The reading took some fifteen minutes in all.

"Well, that's it, I think," the general remarked at last. "How the old explorers used to wonder at the frequency with which such little lost side-branches of civilization appeared to have simply and suddenly ceased to exist!"

He became aware of the colonel's sidelong glance.

"You agree with my interpretation, colonel?"

"Entirely, sir."

The general hesitated. "The population on Ulphi hasn't been too badly debased as yet," he pointed out. "Various reports indicate an I.Q. average of around eleven points

below A-Class—not too bad, considering the early elimination of the strains least acceptable to the controlling mentality and the stultifying effect of life-long general compulsions
on the others.

"They're still eligible for limited membership—capable of
self-government and, with help, of self-defense. It will be
almost a century, of course, before they grow back to a
point where they can be of any real use to us. Meanwhile,
the location of the planet itself presents certain strategic advantages—"

He paused again. "I'm afraid, colonel," he admitted, "that
I'm evading the issue! The fact remains that a case of this
kind simply does not permit of solution by this office. The
identification of Moyuscane the Immortal as the controlling
mentality is safe enough, of course. Beyond that we cannot
take the responsibility for anything but the most general kind
of recommendation. But now, colonel—since I'm an old
man, a cowardly old man who really hates an argument—
I'm going on vacation for the next hour or so.

"Would you kindly confront the Zone Agent with our
findings? I understand she is still waiting on telepath for
them."

Zone Agent Pagadan, however, received the information with a degree of good nature which Colonel Deibos
found almost disquieting.

"Well, if you can't, you can't," she shrugged. "I rather
expected it. The difficulty is to identify our Telep-Two physically without arousing his suspicions? And the danger is
that no one knows how to block things like a planet-wide
wave of suicidal impulses, if he happens to realize that's
a good method of self-defense?"

"That's about it," acknowledged the colonel. "It's very
easy to startle mentalities of his class into some unpredictable aggressive reaction. That makes it a simple matter
to flush them into sight, which helps to keep them from
becoming more than a temporary nuisance, except in such
unsophisticated surroundings as on Ulphi. But in the situation that exists there—when the mentality has established itself and set up a widespread system of controls—it does

demand the most cautious handling on the part of an opera-
tor. This particular case is now further aggravated by the
various psychotic disturbances of Immortalization."

Pagadan nodded. "You're suggesting, I suppose, that the
whole affair should be turned over to Interstellar Crime for
space-scooping or some careful sort of long-range detection like that?"

"It's the method most generally adopted," the colonel said.
"Very slow, of course—I recall a somewhat similar case
which took thirty-two years to solve. But once the directing
mentality has been physically identified without becoming
aware of the fact, it can be destroyed safely enough."

"I can't quite believe in the necessity of leaving Moyuscane in control of that sad little planet of his for another
thirty-two years, or anything like it," the Lannai said slowly.
"I imagine he'll be willing to put up with our presence
until the Bjanta raids have been deflected?"

"That seems to be correct. If you decide to dig him out
yourself, you have about eight weeks to do it. If the Bjantas
haven't returned to Ulphi by then, he'll understand that
they've either quit coming of their own accord, as they
sometimes do—or that they've been chased off secretly.
And he could hardly help hitting on the reason for that!
In either case, the Senate of Ulphi will simply withdraw
its application for membership in the Confederacy. It's no
secret that we're too completely tied up in treaties of nonintervention to do anything but pull our officials out again,
if that's what they want."

"The old boy has it all figured out, hasn't he?" Pagadan
paused. "Well—we'll see. Incidentally, I notice your summation incorporated Lab's report on the space-fear compulsion
Moyuscane's clamped on Ulphi. Do you have that with you
in detail—Lab's report, I mean? I'd like to hear it."

"It's here, yes—" A muted alto voice addressed Pagadan
a moment later:

"In fourteen percent of the neuroplates submitted with
the Agent's report, space-fear traces were found to extend
into the subanalytical levels normally involved in this psychosis. In all others, the symptoms of the psychosis were
readily identifiable as an artificially induced compulsion.

"Such a compulsion would maintain itself under reality-stresses to the point required to initiate space-fear death in the organism but would yield normally to standard treatment."

"Good enough," Pagadan nodded. "Fourteen percent space-fear susceptibility is about normal for that type of planetary population, isn't it? But what about Moyuscane himself? Is there anything to show, anywhere, that he suffered from the genuine brand of the psychosis—that he is one of that fourteen percent?"

"Well—yes, there is!" Colonel Deibos looked a little startled. "That wasn't mentioned, was it? Actually, it shows up quite clearly in the historical note that none of his reported illusion performances had any but planetary backgrounds, and usually interior ones, at that. It's an exceptional Illusionist, you know, who won't play around with deep-space effects in every conceivable variation. But Moyuscane never touched them—"

"Telepath is now cleared for Zone Agent 131.71," the Third Co-ordinator of the Vegan Confederacy murmured into the transmitter before him.

Alone in his office as usual, he settled back into his chair to relax for the few seconds the visualization tank would require to pick up and re-structure Zone Agent Pagadan's personal beam for him.

The office of the Chief of Galactic Zones was as spacious as the control room of a first-line battleship, and quite as compactly equipped with strange and wonderful gadgetry. As the master cell of one of the half dozen or so directing nerve-centers of Confederacy government, it needed it all. The Third Co-ordinator was one of Jeltad's busier citizens, and it was generally understood that no one intruded on his time except for some extremely good and sufficient reason.

However, he was undisturbed by the reflection that there was no obvious reason of any kind for Zone Agent Pagadan's request for an interview. The Lannai was one of the Third Co-ordinator's unofficial group of special Agents, his trouble-shooters de luxe, whom he could and regularly did

unleash in the pits of space against virtually any kind of
opponent—with a reasonable expectation of being informed
presently of the Agent's survival and success. And whenever one of that fast-moving pack demanded his attention,
he took it for granted they had a reason and that it was
valid enough. Frequently, though not always, they would
let him know then what it was.

The transmitter's visualization tank cleared suddenly from
a smokily glowing green into a three-dimensional view of
the *Viper's* control room; and the Co-ordinator gazed with
approval on the silver-eyed, spacesuited, slender figure beyond the ship's massive control desk. Human or not, Pagadan was nice to look at.

"And what do you want now?" he inquired.

"Agent-Trainee Hallerock," the Lannai informed him,
"6972.41, fourth year."

"Hm-m-m. Yes, I know *him!*" The Co-ordinator tapped
the side of his long jaw reflectively. "Rather striking chap,
isn't he?"

"He's beautiful!" Pagadan agreed enthusiastically. "How
soon can you get him out here?"

"Even by Ranger," the Co-ordinator said doubtfully, "it
would be ten days. There's an Agent in the nearest cluster
I could route out to you in just under four."

She shook her head. "Hallerock's the boy—gloomy Hallerock. I met him a few months ago, back on Jeltad," she
added, as if that made it clear. "What are his present estimated chances for graduation?"

The inquiry was strictly counter-regulation, but the Co-
ordinator did not raise an eyebrow. He nudged a switch
on his desk.

"I'll let the psych-tester answer that."

"If the Agent-Trainee were admitted for graduation,"
a deep mechanical voice came immediately from the wall
to his left, "the percentage of probability of his passing all
formal tests would be ninety-eight point seven. But because
of a background conditioned lack of emotional adjustment
to Vegan civilization, graduation has been indefinitely post-
poned."

"What I thought," Pagadan nodded. "Well, just shoot him

out to me then—by Ranger, please!—and I'll do him some good. That's all, and thanks a lot for the interview!"

"It was a pleasure," said the Co-ordinator. Then, seeing her hand move towards her transmitter switch, he added hastily, "I understand you've run into a secondary mission problem out there, and that Correlation foresees difficulties in finding a satisfactory solution."

The Lannai paused, her hand on the switch. She looked a little surprised. "That Ulphian illusionist? Shouldn't be too much trouble. If you're in a hurry for results though, please get behind Lab Supply on the stuff I requisitioned just now—the Hospital ship, the Kynoleen and the special types of medics I need. Push out that, and Hallerock, to me and you'll have my final mission report in three weeks, more or less."

She waved a cheerful farewell and switched off, and the view of the *Viper's* control room vanished from the transmitter.

The Co-ordinator chewed his upper lip thoughtfully.

"Psych-tester," he said then, "just what is the little hell-cat cooking up now?"

"I must remind you," the psych-tester's voice returned, "that Zone Agent 131.71 is one of the thirty-two individuals who have been able to discern my primary purpose here, and who have established temporary blocks against my investigations. She is, furthermore, the first to have established a block so nearly complete that I can offer no significant answer to your question. With that understood, do you wish an estimate?"

"No!" grunted the Co-ordinator. "I'd forgotten. I can make a few wild guesses myself." He ran his hand gently through his graying hair. "Let's see—this Hallerock's trouble is a background conditioned lack of adjustment to our type of civilization, you say?"

"He comes," the psych-tester reminded him, "of the highly clannish and emotionally planet-bound strain of Mark Wieri VI."

The Co-ordinator nodded. "I remember now. Twenty-two thousand light-years out. They've been isolated there almost since the First Stellar Migrations—were rediscovered only a dozen years or so ago. Extra good people! But Hallerock was the only one of them we could talk into going to work for us."

"He appears to be unique among them in being galactic-minded in the Vegan sense," the psych-tester agreed. "Sub-consciously, however, he remains so strongly drawn to his own kind that a satisfactory adjustment to permanent sep-aration from them has not been achieved. Outwardly, the fact is expressed only in a lack of confidence in himself and in those with whom he happens to be engaged in any significant work; but the tendency is so pronounced that it has been considered unsafe to release him for Zonal duty."

"Ninety-eight point seven!" the Co-ordinator said. He swore mildly. "That means he's way the best of the current batch—and I could use a couple like that so beautifully right now! Psychoing won't do it?"

"Nothing short of complete mind-control for a period of several weeks."

The Co-ordinator shook his head. "It would settle his personal difficulties, but he'd be spoiled for us." He con-sidered again, briefly, sighed and decided: "Pagadan's claimed him, anyway. She may wreck him completely; but she knows her therapy at that. Better let her give it a try."

He added, as if in apology:

"I'm sure that if we could consult Trainee Hallercok on the question, he'd agree with us—"

He was reaching out to punch down a desk stud with the last words and continued without a noticeable break:

"Central Communicator clear for Lab report on the rate of spread of the Olleeka plagues—"

His mind clearing also with that of any other matter, he settled back quietly and waited for Lab to come in.

System Chief Jasse, D. C. Cultural Field Investigator, lis-tened attentively till her study recorder had clicked out "Report Dispatched." Then she sat frowning at the gadget for a moment.

The home office would like that report! A brisk, com-petent review of a hitherto obscure section of Ulphi's long-past rough and ready colonial period, pointing out and explaining the contrast between those days and the present quaintly perfect Ulphian civilization. It was strictly in line with the Department of Cultures' view of what any group of A-Class human beings, left to themselves, could achieve and it had sounded plausible enough when she played it back. But somehow it left her dissatisfied. Somehow Ulphi itself left her dissatisfied.

Perhaps she just needed a vacation! As usual, when a new case was keeping her busy, she had been dosing herself with insomniates for the past two weeks. But in her six years of work with Cultures she had never felt the need for a vacation before.

Patting back a yawn in the process of formation, Jasse shook her head, shut off the recorder and stepped out before the study mirror. Almost time for another appointment—some more historical research.

Turning once slowly before the tall mirror, she checked the details of her uniform and its accessories—the Traditionalist Greens which had been taken over with all their symbolic implications by the Department of Cultures. Everything in order, including the concealed gravmoc batteries in belt and boots and the electronic mind-shield switch in her wrist bracelet. No weapons to check; as a matter of policy they weren't carried by D. C. officials.

She pulled a bejeweled cap down on her shoulder-length wave of glossy black hair, grimaced at the face that, at twenty-five or thereabouts, still wore an habitual expression of intent, childish seriousness, and left the study.

By the lake shore, fifty feet from the D. C. mobile-unit's door, the little-people were waiting. Six of them today—middle-aged historians in the long silver-gray garments of their guild, standing beside a beautifully shaped vehicle with a suggestion of breath-taking speed about its lines. The suggestion didn't fool Jasse, who knew by experience that its looks were the only breath-taking thing about an Ulphian flow-car. The best it would produce in action was an air-borne amble, at so leisurely a pace that throughout her first trip in one of the things she had felt like getting out and pushing.

One mustn't, of course, she reminded herself conscientiously, settling back in the flow-car, judge any human culture by the achievements of another! Granted that Ulphi had long since lost the driving power of Vega's humming technologies, who was to say that it hadn't found a better thing in its place?

A fair enough question, but Jasse doubtfully continued to weigh the answer while the lengthy little Ulphian ritual of greetings and expressions of mutual esteem ran its course and came to an end in the flow-car. Then her escort of historical specialists settled down to shop talk in their flowery derivative of one of the twelve basic human dialects, and she began automatically to contribute her visiting dignitary's share to the conversation—just enough to show she was deeply interested but no more. Her attention, however, remained on the city below.

They were gliding only five hundred feet above the lake's shoreline, but all roofs were low enough to permit a wide view—and everything, everywhere, was in superbly perfect symmetry and balance. The car's motion did not change that impression. As it drove on, the gleaming white and softly tinted buildings about and below it flowed steadily into new and always immaculate patterns of sweeping line and blended color, merging in and out of the lake front with a rightness that trembled and stopped at the exact point of becoming too much so.

And that was only a direct visual expression of the essence of Ulphi's culture. Every social aspect of the planet showed the same easy order, the same minute perfectionist precision of graceful living—achieved without apparent effort in cycle on cycle of detail.

Jasse smiled pleasantly at her companions. The puzzling fact remained that this planetary batch of little-people just wasn't particularly bright! And any population with the gumption of a flock of rabbits should have sent a marauding Mother Disk of Bjantas on its way in a panicky hurry, without having to ask for help to solve *that* sort of problem!

She really must need a vacation, Jasse sighed, disturbed by such unorthodox reflections. A-Class humans just didn't go off on the wrong track, however gracefully, unless they were pushed there—so her doubts about Ulphi meant simply that she hadn't found the key to it yet!

Possibly she could do with a few weeks of re-indoctrination in basic Traditionalism.

"The Tomb of Moyuscane the Immortal—the last of our Great Illusionists!"

Jasse regarded the tomb with an air of respectful appreciation. Tombs, on the whole, she could do without; but this one undoubtedly was something special. She and Requada-Attan, Historian and Hereditary Custodian of the Tomb, had come together out of one of the main halls of the enormous building complex which housed the Historical Institute of Ulphi's Central City into a small, transparently over-roofed park. The remainder of her escort had shown her what they had to show and then withdrawn respectfully to their various duties; but Requada-Attan, probably not averse to having a wider audience benefit by the informative lecture he was giving the distinguished visitor, had left the gate to the park open behind them. A small crowd of sightseeing Ulphians had drifted in and was grouped about them by now.

"A fitting resting place for the Immortal One!" Jasse commented piously.

That brought a murmur of general appreciation from the local citizens. She suspected wryly that she, with her towering height and functional Vegan uniform, was the real center of interest in this colorfully robed group of little-people—few of them came up to a point much above the level of her elbows. But otherwise, the Tomb of Moyuscane must seem well worth a visit to a people as culturally self-centered as the Ulphians. Set against the rather conventional background of a green grove and whispering fountains, it was a translucently white monument, combining statelines and exquisite grace with the early sweeping style which the last four centuries had preserved and expanded over the planet.

"The common people have many interesting superstitions about the Tomb," Requada-Attan confided loudly. "They say that Moyuscane's illusions are still to be seen within this park occasionally. Especially at night."

His round, pink face smiled wisely up at her. It was obvious that he, a historical scientist, did not share such superstitions.

Illusion performances, Jasse thought, nodding. She'd seen a few of those of a minor sort herself, but the records indicated that some centuries ago on Ulphi they had been cultivated to an extent which no major civilization would tolerate nowadays. The Illusionists of Ulphi had been priest-entertainers and political leaders; their mental symphonies— a final culmination and monstrous flowering of all the tribal dances and varied body-and-mind shaking communal frenzies of history—had swayed the thinking and the emotional life of the planetary race. And Moyuscane the Immortal had wound up that line of psychic near-rulers as the greatest of them all.

It was rather fascinating at that, she decided, to go adventuring mentally back over the centuries into the realm of a human power which, without word or gesture, could sweep up and blend the emotions of thousands of other human beings into a single mighty current that flowed and ebbed and thundered at the· impulses of one will through the channels its imagination projected.

Fascinating—but a little disturbing, too!

"I think—" she began, and stopped.

Words and phrases which had been no previous part of her thoughts suddenly were floating up in her mind—and now, quite without her volition, she was beginning to utter them!

"But that explains it!" her voice was saying, with a note of pleased, friendly surprise. "I've been wondering about you, Requada-Attan, you and your mysterious, beautiful world! I should have known all along that it was simply the dream-creation of an artist—that one of your Great Illusionists was still alive—"

The last words seemed to drop one by one into a curiously leaden silence, and then they stopped. Jasse was still only completely, incredulously astonished. Then something began to stir in that heavy silence about her; and her head came sharply around.

It was their faces that warned her—once before, she'd

seen the expression of a mob that was acting under mental compulsion; and so she knew at once and exactly what she'd have to do next. Not stop to figure out what had happened, or try to reason with them, argue, threaten, or waste time yelling for help. Just get out of the immediate neighborhood, fast!

There weren't, of course, really enough Ulphians around to be called a mob—hardly more than twenty adults in all. That they had been directed against her was obvious enough, in the eyes that saw only her now, and in the synchronized motion with which they were converging quietly on the spot where she stood.

They stopped moving as if at a command Jasse could not hear, as she swung about, unconsciously with a very similar quietness, to face them.

Requada-Attan was under it, too! He still stood nearest her, about four steps to her left. Straight ahead, between Jasse and the gate, was the next closest group: two husky-looking young men with the shaved heads and yellow robes of professionals from the School of Athletes; and immediately behind them another silver-robed historian whom she had noticed previously—an elderly man, very thin and tall. No weapons in sight anywhere—

The three ahead were the ones to pass then! Jasse took two quick steps in their direction; and gravel scattered instantly under their sandaled feet, as they came to meet her in a rush. All about was the same sudden noise and swirl of motion.

But it was Requada-Attan who reached her first, with a quickness she hadn't counted on in a man of his plump build. Abruptly his weight was dragging at her arm, both hands gripped about her wrist, and jerking sideways to throw her off balance. Jasse twisted free sharply—that wrist carried her mind-shield bracelet and had to be guarded!—hauled the Hereditary Custodian off his feet with her right hand, sent him rolling before the knees of the charging yellow-robes.

They went down in a satisfactorily sprawling confusion, the thin historian turning a complete clumsy somersault with flapping garments across them a moment later. But the others had arrived by then, and Jasse became temporarily the center of a clawing, grappling, hard-breathing but voiceless cluster of humanity. What sent the first shock of real fright through her was that most of them seemed to be trying to get at her shield-bracelet! Because that indicated a mental attack was impending—mental attacks and mass compulsions on present-day Ulphi!

The jolt of that realization—the implication that hidden powers had been roused into action against her on this innocuous-looking world—might have resulted in a rash of snapping necks and other fatal incidents all around Jasse. Though Cultures frowned on weapons for its officials, the ancient Terran Art of the Holds was highly regarded among Traditionalists everywhere and had been developed by them to a polished new perfection. But she hauled herself back promptly from the verge of slipping into that welldrilled routine, which she never yet had put to its devastating practical use. The situation, so far, certainly wasn't as bad as all that—if she just kept her head! Slapping, shoving, shaking and turning, she twisted her way through this temporarily demented group of little-people intent primarily on staying on her feet and keeping her left wrist out of reach.

Then the yellow-robed athletes were up again, and Jasse bumped the two shaven heads together with measured violence, stepped with great caution across an overturned but viciously kicking little boy—found herself suddenly free, and tripped up the last of the lot to come plunging in, a youngish, heavy-set woman.

The brief and practically bloodless melee had circled to within a dozen strides of the gateway of the park. She darted through it, slammed the high bronze gate behind her, saw Requada-Attan's key still in the lock and had her assailants shut in an instant later.

She could spare a moment then to look back at them. Most of them were still on the ground or clambering awkwardly to their feet. With one exception, all stared after her with those chillingly focused and expressionless eyes. The exception was a white-robed, dark-skinned man of middle age with a neatly trimmed fringe of brown beard around

his chin, who stood on a tiled walk a little apart from
the others. He was watching them, and Jasse could not recall
having noticed him before.

Then their eyes met for an instant as she was turning
away, and there was conscious intelligence in his look, min-
gled with something that might have been fright or anger.

At least, she thought, loping worriedly down one of the
corridors towards the main halls of the Institute from which
she had come, she wasn't the only one who had got a
surprise out of the affair! She would have time to think
about that later. The immediate problem was how to get
out of this mess, and it would be stupid to assume that
she had succeeded in that.

There were plenty of other people in those buildings
ahead, and she had no way at all of knowing what their
attitude would be.

She came with swift caution out of the corridor, into a
long, sunbright and apparently deserted hall.

The opposite wall was formed of vertical blue slabs of
some marble-like mineral with wide window embrasures between. The tops of feathery trees and the upper parts of
buildings, a good distance off, were visible beyond the windows. Several hundred feet away in either direction a high
doorway led out of the hall.

Both exits were blocked just now by a wedged, immobile
mass of little-people. Robes of all colors—citizens of all types
and classes, hastily assembled to stop her again. Even at
this distance their faces sickened her. Apparently they had
been directed simply to prevent her from leaving this hall,
until—

It clamped down then about her skull—and tightened!

Mental attack!

Jasse's hands leaped to her temples in a convulsive, involuntary motion, though she knew there was nothing tangi-
ble there to seize. It was inside her, an enormous massing of
tiny, hard pressures which were not quite pain, driving upon
an equal number of critical linkages within her brain. In her
first flash of panicky reaction, it seemed the burst of an

overwhelming, irresistible force. A moment later, she realized it was quite bearable.

She should have known, of course—with her mind-shield activated as it was, it would take some while before that sort of thing could have much effect. The only immediately dangerous part of it was that it cut down the time she could afford to spend on conducting her escape.

She glanced again at the nearer of the two doorways, and knew instantly she wasn't even going to consider fighting her way through another mindless welter of grappling human bodies like that! The nearest window was a dozen steps away.

A full hundred yards beneath her, the building's walls dropped sheer into a big, blue-paved courtyard, with a high-walled park on the opposite side and open to the left on a city street, a block or more away. The street carried a multi-colored, murmuring stream of traffic, too far off to make any immediate difference. A few brightly dressed people were walking across the courtyard below—they made no difference either. The important thing was the row of flow-cars parked against the wall down there, hardly eighty feet to her right.

Her hand dropped to her belt and adjusted the gravmoc unit. She felt almost weightless as she swung over the sill and pushed away from the building; but she touched the pavement in something less than eighteen seconds, rolled over twice and came up running.

There was scattered shouting then. Two young women, about to step out of one of the cars, stared in open-mouthed surprise as she came towards them. But neither they nor anyone else made any attempt to check her departure.

She had one of the vehicles airborne, and headed in the general direction of the lake-front section which was being used as a spaceport by the one Vegan destroyer stationed on Ulphi, before she was reminded suddenly that Central City had police ships for emergency use, which could fly rings around any flow-car—and that long, silvery, dirigiblelike shapes seemed to be riding on guard directly over the area to which she wanted to go!

A few minutes later, she realized the ship might also be several miles to either side of the spaceport. At this distance and altitude she couldn't tell, and the flow-car refused to be urged any higher.

She had kept the clumsy conveyance on its course, because she hadn't really much choice of direction. There was no way of contacting or locating any of the other Vegan officials currently operating on Ulphi except through the destroyer itself or through the communicators in her own study; and her mobile-unit was also in the spaceport area. There were enough similar cars moving about by themselves to keep her from being conspicuous, though traffic, on the whole, was moderate over the city and most of it was confined to fairly definite streams between the more important points.

A second police ship became briefly visible far to her right, gliding close to the building tops and showing hardly more than its silhouette through a light haze which veiled that sector. If they knew where she was, either of the two could intercept her within minutes.

Very probably though, Jasse reassured herself, nobody did know just where she was. The mental force still assailing her shield was non-directional in any spatial sense; and her departure from the Historical Institute must have been much more sudden and swift than had been anticipated by her concealed attackers. In spite of her size, strangers were quite likely to underestimate her because of her slender build and rather childlike features, and on occasions like this that could be very useful. But—

Jasse bit her lip gently, conscious of a small flurry of panic bubbling up inside her and subsiding again, temporarily.

Because they needed only to ring off the spaceport, far enough away from the destroyer to avoid arousing its interest, and then wait for her arrival. She would have to come to them then—and soon! Her shield was still absorbing the punishment it was getting, but secondary effects of that unrelenting pressure had begun to show up. The barest touch of a dozen different, slowly spreading sensations within her brain—burning, tingling, constricting, dully throbbing sensations. Within the last few minutes, the first flickering traces of visual and auditory disturbances had appeared. Effects like that could build up for an indeterminate time without doing any real damage. But in the end they would merge suddenly into an advanced stage of blurred confusion —technically, her shield might still maintain its function; but she would no longer know or be able to control what she did.

A curiously detached feeling overcame Jasse then as the flow-car carried her steadily forward into whatever lay ahead. What she had to do was clear enough: go on until she was discovered and then ground the flow-car and try her luck on foot. But meanwhile, who or what had stirred up this mess about her? What were they after?

She sat quietly behind the flow-car's simple controls, leaning forward a trifle to conceal herself, while her mind ran over the implications of the odd little speech she had made in the park before Moyuscane's tomb. Those hadn't been her thoughts; if they had been, she wouldn't have uttered them voluntarily—so, shielded or not, somebody must have been tampering with her mind before this! Were there opposing groups of mental adepts on Ulphi, and was one of them trying to use her, and Vega, against the other in some struggle for control of this planetary civilization?

Once more then, System Chief Jasse surprised herself completely—this time by a flash of furious exasperation with the lofty D. C. policies which had put her in a spot like this unarmed. To trust in the innate rightness of A-Class humanity was all very well. But, mysterious superior mentalities or not, a good, ordinary, old-fashioned blaster in her hand would have been *so* satisfactory just now!

"Oh, Suns and Planets!" Jasse muttered aloud, shocked into a half-forgotten Traditionalist invocation acquired during her childhood. "They've got me fighting mad!"

And at that moment, a clean-edged shadow, which was not the shadow of any cloud, came sliding soundlessly over the flow-car and stayed there.

Jasse, heart pounding wildly, was still trying to twist around far enough to look up without pitching herself out of the car or releasing its controls when a voice, some twenty feet above her, remarked conversationally:

"Say—I thought it was you!"

She stared up speechlessly.

The words had been Vegan—and nothing like that dull-green, seamless, thirty-foot sliver of space-alloy floating overhead had ever been dreamed up on Ulphi! While the pert, huge-eyed face that peered down at her out of the craft's open lock—she remembered suddenly the last time she'd met that member of a nonhuman race in a G. Z. space-duty uniform and the polite effort she'd made to mask the antipathy and suspicions which were bound to arise in a Traditionalist when confronted by any such half-and-half creature.

But—safe!

A shaking began in her knees. She sat down quietly.

And Zone Agent Pagadan, for whom any kind of thought-shield on which she really directed her attention became as sheerest summer gossamer—unless, of course, it was backed by a mind that approximated her own degree of nerve-energy control—smiled amiably and chalked one up to her flair for dramatic timing.

"Remember me, eh?" she nodded. "Pelial, of Galactic Zones, at your service! I was scoping the area from ten miles above and spotted you drifting along by yourself. What occurs, my tall colleague? Are you just going sight-seeing in that piece of primitive craftsmanship, or did your pilot fall out?"

"Ulp—!" began Jasse, nodding and shaking her head at the same time. Pagadan's contemplative eyes became a little bigger.

"Skip it!" she said apprehensively. "From close up, you look both chewed on and distraught, my girl! What happ—Hey, hang on a moment and I'll slide in close and take you aboard. Maybe you ought to be home in bed, or something."

The head withdrew; and Jasse took a deep, sighing breath, raked a snarled strand of black hair out of her forehead and dabbed tentatively at a deep scratch on the back of her hand.

She did look a mess, now that she noticed it—the Greens were badly ripped and streaked with the blue chalk of the pavement over which she had rolled; and her jeweled cap was gone. A moment passed before she realized suddenly that the clinging constrictions of the mental attack were gone, too!

She was still wondering about that as she swung over into the space-skiff, steadied by Pagadan's gloved hand.

Then, as the skiff's lock slammed shut behind her, she made another discovery:

Her shield-bracelet hung free, attached to her wrist now only by its safety chain. The shield switch flickered, warningly red, on "Open"—

"Your mind-shield?" The Lannai Agent, measuring a rose-colored liquid carefully from a fat little jug into a cup, absently repeated Jasse's stunned exclamation. "Probably snagged the bracelet while you were climbing in from the car. It happens." She glanced around and her eyes caught the light with a wicked crystalline glitter. "Why? Could it matter? Was someone pressuring you?"

"They were before," Jasse whispered; and suddenly there wasn't any question about her being frightened! Panic hammered into her brain and stayed; a dizzy shimmering grew before her eyes. Mixed with that came a queer, growing feeling as if something were surging and pulsing within her skull—a wildly expectant feeling of *something* about to happen.

She realized the Lannai was holding the filled cup to her lips.

"Drink that!" the cool voice ordered. "Whatever you've got it's good for. Then just settle back, relax, and let's hear what you know!"

The liquid she had gulped, Jasse noticed, wasn't really rose-colored as she had thought, but a deep, dim, ruby red, almost black—an enormously *quiet* color—and with a highly curious slowing-down effect on things, too! For instance, you might realize perfectly well that somewhere, out around the edges of you, you were still horribly upset, with fear-thoughts racing about everywhere at a dizzy speed. Every so often, one of them would turn inwards and come shooting right at you, flashing like a freezing arrow into the deep-red dusk where you were. But just as you started to shrink away from it, you noticed it was getting slower and slower, the farther it came; until finally it just stayed where it was, and then gradually melted away.

They never could get through to reach you. It was rather comical!

It appeared she had asked some question about it, because the big-eyed little humanoid was saying:

"You like the effect, eh? That's just antishock, little chum! Thought you knew the stuff . . . don't they teach you anything at Cultures?"

That was funny, too! Cultures, of course, taught you everything there was to know! But wait—hadn't there been . . . what had there been that she—? Jasse decided to examine that point about Cultures very carefully, some other time.

By and large there seemed to be a good deal of quiet conversation going on around her. Perhaps she was doing some of it, but it was hard to tell; since, frankly, she wasn't much interested in those outside events any more. And then, for a while, the two tall shapes, the man and the woman, came up again to the barrier in her past and tried to talk to her, as they always did when she was feeling anxious and alone. A little puzzled, because she didn't feel that way now, Jasse watched them from her side of the barrier, which was where the explosions and shrieking lights were, that had brought terror and hurt and the sudden forgetting which none of Culture's therapists had been able to lift. Dimly, she could sense the world behind them, to which they wanted her to go—the star-glittering cold and the great silent flows of snow, and the peace and enchantment that were there. But she could make no real effort to reach it now, and in the end the tall shapes seemed to realize that and went away.

Or else, they merely faded out of her sight as the color

about her deepened ever more from ruby redness into the ultimate, velvety, all-quieting, all-slowing-down *black*—

"Wonderful—" Jasse murmured contentedly, asleep.

"Hallerock?"

"Linked in, Pag! I'm back on the Observation Ship again.
Go ahead."

"Just keep this thought-line down tight! Everything's working like a charm, so far. I tripped the D. C.'s shield open
when I took her aboard, and our good friend Moyuscane
came right in, all set to take control and find out whether
we actually knew something about him and his setup here
or not. Then he discovered I was around, and he's been
lying quiet and just listening through her ever since."

"What makes him shy of you?" Hallerock inquired.

"He tried a long-range probe at my shields a couple of
weeks ago. I slapped him on the beak—some perfectly
natural startled-reaction stuff by another telepath, you understand. But he certainly didn't like it! He went out fast,
that time—"

"I don't blame him," Hallerock said thoughtfully. "Sometimes you don't realize your own strength. Does the D. C.
really have anything on him?"

"No. It's about as we suspected. She made some sort of
innocent remark—I couldn't take the chance of digging
around in her mind long enough to find out just what—and
Moyuscane jumped to the wrong conclusions."

"I was wondering, you know," Hallerock admitted,
"whether you mightn't have done some work on the Cultures
girl in advance—something that would get her to drop a
few bricks at some appropriate occasion."

"Well, you're just naturally a suspicious little squirt!" Pagadan replied amiably. "To use Confederacy personnel against
their will and knowledge for any such skulduggery is strictly
counter-regulation. I advise you to make a note of the
fact! However, it was the luckiest sort of coincidence. It
should save us a week or two of waiting, especially since
you have the hospital ship and staff all prepared. Moyuscane's got himself a listening-post right in our ranks now,
and that's all he needs to stay reasonably safe—he thinks!"

Hallerock appeared to be digesting this information for a moment. Then his thought came again:

"Where are you at present?"

"Down at the Central City spaceport, still in the *Viper's* skiff. The D. C.'s under antishock and asleep on the bunk here."

"Oh," said Hallerock, "you're all ready to start the drive then?"

"Wake up, little brother!" Pagadan advised him. It started ten minutes ago! The last thing I told the girl before she went down deep was that a Vegan Fleet Hospital Ship was approaching Ulphi with a brand-new, top-secret drug against space-fear, called Kynoleen—a free gift from the Confederacy to the afflicted population of this planet."

"Well . . . I suppose I'd better set the H-Ship down at the spaceport about an hour from now, then?"

"One hour would be about right. Moyuscane must be in a considerable stew at the prospect of having the Kynoleen disclose the fact that most of the local population is suffering from an artificially imposed space-fear psychosis, but it won't take him long to see to it that the drug won't actually be used around here for quite some time. When that's settled, we'll let him breathe easier for about three hours. Then I'll wake up the D. C., make sure he's listening through her and feed him the *big* jolt. So see I get that message we've prepared half an hour beforehand—three hours and thirty minutes from now! And send it as a straight coded communication, to make it look authentic."

"All right," Hallerock said doubtfully. "But wouldn't it be better to check over the entire schedule once more—just to be sure nothing can go wrong?"

"There's no need for that!" the Lannai said, surprised. "We've got Moyuscane analyzed down to the length of his immortal whiskers, and we've worked out the circumstances required to produce the exact effects we want. It's just a matter of timing it now. You're not letting yourself get rattled by a Telepath of the Second Order, are you? If he didn't happen to have the planet under control, this wouldn't be a job for Galactic Zones at all."

"Possibly not," said Hallerock reasonably, "but then he

does have it under control. Enough to hash it up from one pole to the other if he panics. That's what keeps putting this dew on my brow."

"Agent-Trainee Hallerock," Pagadan replied impatiently, "I love you like a son or something, but at times you talk like a dope. Even a Telep-Two doesn't panic, unless you let him get the idea he's cornered. All we've got to do is keep Moyuscane's nose pointed towards the one way out and give him time enough to use it when we switch on the pressure— but not quite time enough to change his mind again. If it makes you feel any better, you could put trackers on any unprotected Vegans for the next eight hours."

Hallerock laughed uneasily. "I just finished doing that," he admitted.

Pagadan shrugged. Gloomy old Hallerock! From here on out, he'd be waiting for the worst to happen, though this kind of a job, as anyone who had studied his training records would know, was right up his alley. And it had been a pleasure, at that, to observe the swift accuracy with which he'd planned and worked out the schedule and details of this operation, in spite of head-shakings and forebodings. The only thing he couldn't possibly have done was to take the responsibility for it himself.

She smiled faintly, and came over to sit down for a while beside the bunk on which Jasse was lying.

Two hours later, when her aide contacted her again, he seemed comparatively optimistic.

"Reaction as predicted," he reported laconically. "I'm beginning to believe you might know what you're doing."

"Moyuscane's got the Kynoleen space-tests stalled?"

"Yes. The whole affair was hushed up rather neatly. The H-Ship is down now at some big biochemical center five hundred miles from Central City, and the staff was routed through to top officials immediately. The question was raised then whether Ulphian body chemistry mightn't have varied just far enough from standard A-Class to make it advisable to conduct a series of local lab experiments with the drug before putting it to use. Our medics agreed and were asked, as between scientists, to keep the matter quiet meanwhile, to avoid exciting the population unduly. There also was the expected vagueness as to how long the experiments might take."

"It makes it so much easier," Pagadan said gratefully, "when the opposition is using its brains! Was anyone shown around the ship?"

"A few dozen types of specialists are still prowling all over it. They've been introduced to our personnel. It seems a pretty safe bet," Hallerock acknowledged hesitantly, "that Moyuscane has discovered there isn't a shielded mind among them, and that he can take control of the crate and its crew whenever he wants." He paused. "So now we just wait a while?"

"And let him toy around with the right kind of ideas," agreed Pagadan. "He should be worried just enough by now to let them come floating up naturally."

Night had fallen over Central City when the message she was expecting was rattled suddenly from the skiff's communicator. She decoded it, produced evidence of considerable emotional shock, shook Jasse awake and, in a few dozen suitably excited sentences, handed Moyuscane his jolt. After that, though, there were some anxious moments before she got her patient quieted down enough to let the antishock resume its over-all effect.

"She kept wanting to get up and do something about it!" Pagadan reported to Hallerock, rubbing a slightly sprained wrist. "But I finally got it across that it wasn't Cultures' job to investigate undercover mass homicide on a foreign planet, and that one of our own Zone Agents, no less, was landing secretly tomorrow to take charge of the case."

"And that," said Hallerock darkly, "really *is* switching on the pressure!"

"Just pressure enough for our purpose. It's still a big, hidden organization that's suspected of those fancy murder rituals, and not just one little telepath who's played at being planetary god for the past few centuries. Of course, if we'd pointed a finger straight at Moyuscane himself, he would have cracked right there."

She passed a small handkerchief once, quickly, over her forehead. "This kind of thing is likely to be a bit nerve-wracking until you get used to it," she added reassuringly. "I can remember when I've felt just about as jumpy as you're feeling now. But all we have to do is to settle down and let Moyuscane work out his little problem by himself. He can't help seeing the answer—"

But a full two hours passed then, and the better part of a third, while Pelial, the minor official of Galactic Zones, continued to work quietly at her files of reports and recordings, and received and dispatched various coded communications connected with the impending arrival of her superior— the hypothetical avenging Zone Agent.

By now, she conceded at last, she might be beginning to feel a little disturbed, though, naturally, she had prepared alternative measures, in case—

Hallerock's thought flashed questioningly into her mind then. For a moment, Pagadan stopped breathing.

"Linked!" she told him crisply. "Go ahead!"

"The leading biochemists of Ulphi," Hallerock informed her, "have just come up with a scientific achievement that would be regarded as noteworthy almost anywhere—"

"You subhuman comic!" snapped Pagadan. *"Tell* me!"

". . . Inasmuch as they were able to complete—analyze, summarize and correlate—all tests required to establish the complete harmlessness of the new space-fear drug Kynoleen for all type variations of Ulphian body-chemistry. They admit that, to some extent, they are relying—"

"Hallerock," Pagadan interrupted, in cold sincerity now, "you drag in one more unnecessary detail, and the very next time I meet you, you're going to be a great, big, ugly-looking dead body!"

"That's not like you, Pag!" Hallerock complained. "Well, they rushed fifty volunteers over to the H-Ship anyway, to have Kynoleen given a final check in space right away—all Ulphi is now to have the benefit of it as soon as possible. But nobody seemed particularly upset when our medics reminded them they had been informed that the ship was equipped to conduct tests on only *one* subject at a time—"

Pagadan drew a shivery breath and sat suffused for a moment by a pure, bright glow of self-admiration.

"When will they take off with him?" she inquired with quiet triumph.

"They took off ten minutes ago," her aide returned innocently, "and headed straight out. As a matter of fact, just before I beamed you, the test-subject had discovered that ten minutes in space will get you a whole lot farther than any Telep-Two can drive a directing thought. It seemed to disturb him to lose contact with Ulphi—WOW! Watch it, Pag! Supposing I hadn't been shielded when that lethal stunner of yours landed!"

"That's a beautiful supposition!" hissed Pagadan. "Some day, you won't be! But the planet's safe, anyway—I guess I can forgive you. And now, my friend, you may start worrying about the ship!"

"I've got to compliment you," she admitted a while later, "on the job you did when you installed those PT-cells. What I call perfect coverage! Half the time I don't know myself from just what point of the ship I'm watching the show."

She was curled up now in a large chair, next to the bunk on which Jasse still slumbered quietly; and she appeared almost as completely relaxed as her guest. The upper part of her head was covered by something like a very large and thick-walled but apparently light helmet, which came down over her forehead to a line almost with her eyes, and her eyes were closed.

"Just at the moment"—Hallerock hesitated—"I think you're using the Peeping Tommy in the top left corner of the visitank Moyuscane's looking into. He still doesn't really like the idea of being out in deep space, does he?"

"No, but he's got his dislike of it under control," Pagadan said lazily. "He's the one," she added presently, "who directed the attack on our D. C. today at the Historical Institute. She has a short but very sharp memory-picture of him. So it *is* Moyuscane, all right!"

"You mean," Hallerock asked, stunned, "you weren't really sure of it?"

"Well—you can't ever be *sure* till everything's all over," Pagadan informed him cheerfully. "And then you sometimes wonder." She opened her eyes, changed her position in the chair and settled back carefully again. "Don't you pass out on me, Hallerock!" she warned. "You're supposed to be recording every single thing that happens on the H-Ship for Lab!"

There hadn't been, Hallerock remarked, apparently still somewhat disturbed, very much to record as yet. The dark-skinned, trimly bearded Ulphian volunteer was, of course, indulging in a remarkable degree of activity, considering he'd been taken on board solely as an object of scientific investigation. But no one about him appeared to find anything odd in that. Wherever he went, padding around swiftly on bare feet and dressed in a set of white hospital pajamas, the three doctors who made up the ship's experimental staff followed him earnestly, with a variety of instruments at the ready, rather like a trio of mother hens trailing an agitated chicken. Occasionally, they interrupted whatever he was doing and carried out some swift examination or other, to which he submitted indifferently.

But he spoke neither to them nor to any of the ship's officers he passed. And they, submerged in their various duties with an intentness which alone might have indicated that this was no routine flight, appeared unaware of his presence.

"The old boy's an organizer," Pagadan conceded critically. "He's put a flock of experts to work for him, and he's smart enough to leave them alone. They've got the ship on her new course by now, haven't they? Can you make out where they think they're going?"

Hallerock told her.

"An eighty-three day trip!" she said thoughtfully. "Looks like he didn't want to have anything at all to do with us any more! Someone on board must know what's in that region —or was able to get information on it."

Up to the end, that was almost all there was to see. At a velocity barely below the cruising speed of a Vegan destroyer, the H-Ship moved away from Ulphi. Like a harried executive, too involved in weighty responsibilities to bother about his informal attire, the solitary Ulphian continued to roam about within the ship, disregarded by all but his attendant physicians. But finally—he was back in the ship's big control room by then and had just cast another distasteful glance at the expanse of star-glittering blackness within the visitank between the two pilots—Moyuscane began to speak.

It became startlingly clear in that instant how completely alone he actually was among the H-Ship's control crew. Like a man who knows he need not act with restraint in a dream peopled by phantoms, the ex-ruler of Ulphi poured forth what was in his mind, in a single screaming spurt of frustrated fury and fears and hopes that should have swung the startled attention of everybody within hearing range upon him, like the sudden ravings of a madman.

The pilots became involved with the chief navigator and his two assistants in à brisk five-cornered discussion of a stack of hitherto unused star-plates. The three doctors— gathered about the couch on which Moyuscane sat—exchanged occasional comments with the calm unhurriedness of men observing the gradual development of a test, the satisfactory conclusion of which already is assured.

As suddenly as the outburst had begun, it was over. The Ulphian wiped his mouth with the back of his hand, and sat scowling quietly at the floor.

"I think," said Pagadan, "you could start the destroyers out after them now, Hallerock!"

"I just did," Hallerock said. "I clocked the end of 'minimum effective period' right in the middle of that little speech."

"So did I," she replied. "And I hope it won't be too long now. I've got work to do here, and it shouldn't wait."

There were sufficiently deadly gadgets of various types installed throughout the fugitive ship, which they could have operated through the PT-cells. But since all of them involved some degree of risk to the ship's personnel they were intended for emergency use only—in case Moyuscane attempted to vent his annoyance with the change in his worldly fortunes on one of his new subjects. Pagadan, however, had not believed that the recent lord of all Ulphi would be capable of wasting any part of his reduced human resources for any motive so impractical as spite.

Convinced by now that she was right in that, she waited, more patiently on the whole than Hallerock, for something safer than gun or gas to conclude Moyuscane's career.

It caught up with him some twenty minutes later—something that touched him and went through him in a hardly perceptible fashion, like the twitching of a minor electric shock.

The reaction of the two watchers was so nearly simultaneous that neither knew afterwards which of them actually tripped the thought-operated mechanism which filled the H-Ship briefly with a flicker of cold radiation near the upper limit of visibility for that particular crew.

To that signal, the ship's personnel reacted in turn, though in a far more leisurely manner. They blinked about doubtfully for a few seconds as if trying to remember something; and then—wherever they were and whatever they happened to be doing—they settled down deliberately on chairs, bunks, beds, and the floor, stretched out, and went to sleep.

Moyuscane alone remained active, since his nerve centers had not been drenched several days before with a catalyst held there in suspense until that flare of radiance should touch it off. Almost within seconds though, he was plucked out of his appalled comprehension of the fact that there was no longer a single mind within his reach that would respond to control. For Kynoleen gave complete immunity to space-fear within the time limit determined by the size of the dose and the type of organism affected, but none at all thereafter. And whatever the nature of the shattering terrors the hidden mechanisms of the mind flung up when gripped in mid-space by that dreaded psychosis, their secondary effects on body and brain were utterly devastating.

Swiftly and violently, then, Moyuscane the Immortal died, some four centuries after his time, bones and muscles snapping in the mounting fury of the Fear's paroxysms. Hallerock, still conscientiously observing and recording for G. Z. Lab's omnivorous files, felt somewhat sick. But Pagadan appeared undisturbed.

"I'd have let him out an easier way if it could have been done safely," her thought came indifferently. "But he would, after all, have considered this barely up to his own standards of dispatch. Turn the ship back now and let the destroyers pick it up, will you, Hallerock? I'll be along to see you after a while—"

The *Viper* came slamming up behind the Observation Ship some five hours later, kicked it negligently out of its orbit around Ulphi, slapped on a set of tractors fore and aft, and hauled it in, lock to lock.

"Just thirty-five seconds ago," Hallerock informed Pagadan coldly as she trotted into the O-Ship's control room, "every highly condemned instrument on this unusually condemned crate got knocked clean out of alignment! Any suggestion as to what might have caused it?"

"Your language, my pet!" Pagadan admonished, for his actual phrasing had been more crisp. She flipped a small package across his desk into his hands. "To be studied with care immediately after my departure! But you might open it now."

A five-inch cube of translucence made up half the package. It contained the full-length image of a slender girl with shining black hair, who carried a javelin in one hand and wore the short golden skirt of a contestant in the planetary games of Jeltad.

"Cute kid!" Hallerock acknowledged. "Vegan, eh? The rest of it's a stack of her equation-plates? Who is she and what do I do about it?"

"That's our Department of Cultures investigator," Pagadan explained.

"The System Chief?" Hallerock said surprised. He glanced at the image again, which was a copy of one of Snoops' three-dimensionals, and looked curiously up at the Lannai. "Didn't you just finish doing a mental job on her?"

"In a way. Mostly a little hypno-information to bring her up to date on what's been going on around Ulphi—including her part in it. She was asleep in that D. C. perambulator she's camping in here when I left her."

"As I understand it," Hallerock remarked thoughtfully, "the recent events on Ulphi would be classified as information very much restricted to Galactic Zones! So you wouldn't have spotted the makings of a G. Z. parapsychic mind in a D. C. System Chief, would you?"

"Bright boy! I'll admit it's an unlikely place to look for one, but she *is* a type we can use. I'm releasing her now for G. Z. information, on Agent authority. Her equation-plates will tell you how to handle her in case she runs into emotional snags while absorbing it. You're to be stationed on Ulphi another four months anyway, and you're to consider that a high-priority part of your job."

"I will? Another four months?" Hallerock repeated incredulously. "I was winding up things on the O-Ship to start back to Jeltad. You don't need me around here any more, do you?"

"I don't, no!" Pagadan appeared to be quietly enjoying herself. "The point is though, I'm the one who's leaving. Got word from Central two hours ago to report back at speed, just as soon as we'd mopped up Old Man Moyuscane."

"What for?" Hallerock began to look bewildered. "The Agent work isn't finished here."

She shook her head. "Don't know myself yet! But it's got to do with the recordings on those pickled Bjantas you homed back to Lab. Central sounded rather excited." The silver eyes were sparkling with unconcealed delight now. "It's to be a Five-Agent Mission, Hallerock!" she fairly sang. "Beyond Galactic Rim!"

"Beyond the Rim? For Bjanta? They've got something really new on them then!" Hallerock had come to his feet.

Pagadan nodded and smacked her lips lightly. "Sounds like it, doesn't it? New and conclusive—and we delivered it to them! But now look what a face it's making," she added maliciously, "just because it doesn't get to go along!"

Hallerock scowled and laughed. "Well, I've been wondering all this time about those Bjantas. Now you take out after them—and I can hang around Ulphi dishing out a little therapy to a D. C. neurotic."

"We all start out small," said the Lannai. "Look at me— would you believe that a few short years ago I was nothing but the High Queen of Lar-Sancaya? Not," she added loyally, "that there's a sweeter planet anywhere, from the Center to the Clouds or beyond!"

"And that stretch distinctly includes Ulphi," Hallerock stated, unreconciled to his fate. "When's the new Agent coming out to this hive of morons?"

Pagadan slid to her feet off the edge of the desk and surveyed him pityingly. "You poor chump! What I gave you just now was Advance Mission Information, wasn't it? Ever hear of a time that wasn't restricted to Zone Agent levels? Or do I have to tell you officially that you've just finished putting in a week as a Z. A. under orders?"

Hallerock stared at her. His mouth opened and shut and opened again. "Here, wait a—" he began.

She waved him into silence with both fists.

"Close it kindly, and listen to the last instructions I'm giving you! Ulphi's being taken in as a Class 18 System—outpost garrison. I imagine even you don't have to be told that the only thing not strictly routine about the procedure will be the elimination of every traceable connection between its present culture and Moyuscane's personal influence on it—and our recent corrective operation?"

"Well, of course!" Hallerock said hoarsely. "But look here, Pag—"

"Considerable amount of detail work in that, naturally—it's why the monitors at Central have assigned you four whole months for the job. When you're done here, report back to Jeltad. They've already started roughing out your robot, but they'll need you around to transfer basic impulse patterns and so on. A couple of months more, and you'll be equipped for any dirty work they can think up—and I gather the Chief's already thought up some sweet ones especially for you! So God help you—and now I'm off. Unless you've got some more questions?"

Hallerock looked at her, his face impassive now. If she had been human he couldn't have told her. But, unlike most of the men of Pagadan's acquaintance, Hallerock never forgot that the Lannai were of another kind. It was one of the things she liked about him.

"No, I haven't any questions just now," he said. "But if I'm put to work by myself on even a job like this, I'm going to feel lost and alone. I just don't have the feeling that I can be trusted with Z. A. responsibility."

Pagadan waved him off again, impatiently.

"The feeling will grow on you," she assured him.

And then she was gone.

As motion and velocity were normally understood, the *Viper's* method of homeward progress was something else again. But since the only exact definition of it was to be found in a highly complex grouping of mathematical concepts, such terms would have to do.

She was going home, then, at approximately half her normal speed, her automatic receptors full out. Pagadan sat at her desk, blinking reflectively into the big vision tank, while she waited for a call that had to be coming along any moment now.

She felt no particular concern about it. In fact, she could have stated to the minute how long it would take Hallerock to recover far enough from the state of slight shock she'd left him in to reach out for the set of dossier-plates lying on his desk. A brief section of System Chief Jasse's recent behavior-history, with the motivation patterns underlying it, was revealed in those plates, in the telepathic shorthand which turned any normally active hour of an individual's life into as complete a basis for analysis as ordinary understanding required.

She'd stressed that job just enough to make sure he'd attend to it before turning to any other duties. And Hallerock was a quick worker. It should take him only three or four minutes to go through the plates, the first time.

But then he'd just sit there for about a minute, frowning down at them, looking a little baffled and more than a little worried. Poor old Hallerock! Now he couldn't even handle a simple character-analysis any more unaided!

Grimly he'd rearrange the dossier-plates, tap them together into a neat little pile, and start all over again. He'd go through each one very slowly and carefully now, determined to catch the mistake that *had* to be there!

Pagadan grinned faintly.

Almost to the calculated second, his search-thought came flickering after her down the curving line to Jeltad. As the

Viper's receptors caught it and brought it in, she flipped over
the transmitter switch:

"Linked, Hallerock—nice reach you've got! What gives,
my friend?"

There was a short pause; then:

"Pag, what's wrong with her—the D. C., I mean?"

"Wrong with her?" Pagadan returned, on a note of mild
surprise.

"In the plates," Hallerock explained carefully. "She's an
undeveloped parapsychic, all right—a Telep-Three, at the
least. But she's also under a master-delusion—thinks she's a
physical monster of some kind! Which she obviously isn't."

The Lannai hesitated, letting a trickle of uncertainty
through to him to indicate a doubtful mental search. There
wasn't, after all, anything that took quite such ticklish,
sensitive handling as a parapsychic mind that had gone
thoroughly off the beam.

"Oh, that!" she said, suddenly and obviously relieved.
"That's no delusion, Hallerock—just one of those typical
sub-level exaggerations. No doubt I overemphasized it a
little. There's nothing wrong with her really—she's A-Class
plus. Very considerably plus, as you say. But she's not a
Vegan."

"Not a Vegan? Well, why should—"

"And, of course, she's always been quite sensitive about
that physical peculiarity!" Pagadan resumed, with an air of
happy discovery. "Even as a child. But with the Traditionalist
training she was getting, she couldn't consciously admit any
awareness of isolation from other human beings. It's just
that our D. C.'s a foundling, Hallerock. I should have mentioned it, I suppose. They picked her up in space, and she's
of some unidentified human breed that grows around eight
foot tall—"

Back in the study of her mobile-unit, System Chief Jasse
wiped her eyes, blew her nose, and pocketed her handkerchief decisively.

She'd blubbered for an hour after she first woke up. The
Universe of the Traditionalists had been such a nice, tidy,
easy-to-understand place to live in, even if she'd never felt

completely at her ease there! It had its problems to be met and solved, of course; and there were the lesser, nonhuman races, to be coolly pitied for their imperfections and kept under control for their own good, and everybody else's. But that A-Class humanity could work itself into such a dismally gruesome mess as it had done on Ulphi—that just wasn't any part of the Traditionalist picture! They didn't want any such information there. They could live more happily without it.

Well, let them live happily then! She was still Jasse, the spaceborn, and in return for knocking down the mental house of cards she'd been living in, the tricky little humanoid at any rate had made her aware of some unsuspecting possibilities of her own which she could now develop.

She began to re-examine those discoveries about herself with a sort of new, cool, speculating interest. There were two chains of possibilities really—that silent, cold, whitely enchanted world of her childhood dreams came floating up in her mind again, clear and distinct under its glittering night-sky now that the barriers that had blurred it in her memory had been dissolved. The home-world of her distant race! She could go to it if she chose, straight and unerringly, and find the warm human strength and companionship that waited there. That knowledge had been returned to her, too.

But was that what she wanted most?

There was another sort of companionship, the Lannai had implied, and a different sort of satisfaction she could gain, beyond that of placidly living out her life among her own kind on even the most beautiful of frozen worlds. They were constructing a civilized galaxy just now, and they would welcome her on the job.

She'd bathed, put on a fresh uniform and was pensively waiting for her breakfast to present itself from the wall-butler in the study, when the unit's automatic announcer addressed her:

"Galactic Zones Agent Hallerock requesting an interview."

Jasse started and half turned in her chair to look at the closed door. Now what did that mean? She didn't want to see any of *them* just yet! She intended to make up her own mind on the matter.

She said, a little resentfully:

"Well . . . let him right in, please!"

The study door opened as she flipped the lock-switch on her desk. A moment later, Hallerock was bowing to her from the entrance hall just beyond it.

Jasse began to rise, glanced up at him; and then sat back suddenly and gave him another look.

"Hello, Jasse!" Hallerock said, in a voice that sounded amiable but remarkably self-assured.

Even when not set off as now by his immaculate blue and white G. Z. dress uniform, Zone Agent Hallerock undoubtedly was something almost any young woman would look at twice. However, it wasn't so much that he was strikingly handsome with his short-cropped dark-red hair and the clear, black-green eyes with their suggestion of some icy midnight ocean. The immediate point was that you didn't have to look twice to know that he came from no ordinary planet of civilization.

Jasse got up slowly from behind her desk and came around it and stood before Hallerock.

Basically, that was it perhaps—the world he came from! Mark Wieri VI, a frontier-type planet, so infernally deserving of its classification that only hare-brained first-stage Terrans would have settled there in the first place. Where the equatorial belt was a riot of throbbing colors, a maddened rainbow flowering and ripening, for two months of a thirty-eight month year—and then, like the rest of that bleak world forever, sheet-ice and darkness and the soundless, star-glittering cold.

Even back on Terra, two paths had been open to life that faced the Great Cold as its chosen environment. To grow squalidly tough, devoted to survival in merciless single-mindedness—or to flourish into a triumphant excess of strength that no future challenge could more than half engage.

On Mark Wieri's world, human life had adapted, inevitably, to its relentlessly crushing environment. In the two hundred and eighty-odd generations between the last centuries of the First Stellar Migrations and the day an ex-

ploring Giant-Ranger of the Confederacy turned in that direction, it had become as much a part of its background as
the trout is of its pool. And no more than the trout could it
see any purpose in leaving so good a place again.

But it had not, in any sense, grown squalid.

So Jasse stood before Hallerock, and she was still looking
up at him. There were nine foot three inches of him to look
up to, shaped into four hundred and sixty-five lean pounds
of tigerish symmetry.

The dress uniform on a duty call was a clue she didn't
miss or need. The ice of his home-planet was in Hallerock's
eyes; but so was the warm, loyal human strength that had
triumphed over it and carelessly paid in then the full, final
price of conquest. This son of the conquerors alone had been
able to sense that the galaxy itself was now just wide and
deep and long enough for man; and so he'd joined the
civilization that was of a like spirit.

But he, too, had been a giant among little-people then. If
his conscious thoughts wouldn't admit it, every cell of his
body knew he'd lost his own kind.

Jasse, all her mind groping carefully, questioningly out towards this phenomenon, this monster-slayer of Galactic
Zones—beginning to understand all that and a good deal
more—slowly relaxed again.

A kinsman of hers! Her own eyes began to smile, finally.
"Hello, Hallerock!" Jasse said.

And that was, Pagadan decided, about the right moment to
dissolve the PT-cell she'd spent an hour installing in the wall
just above the upper right-hand corner of Jasse's study mirror.

Those two baby giants might be all full of emotional flut-
ters just now at having met someone from the old home
town; but they were going to start thinking of their good
friend Pagadan almost immediately! And one of the very first
things that would leap to Hallerock's suspicious mind would
be the possible presence of a Peeping Tommy.

Good thing those tiny units left no detectable trace!

She pulled off the PT-helmet, yawned delicately and sat
relaxed for a minute, smirking reminiscently into the vision-
tank.

"What I call a really profitable mission!" she informed the vision-tank. "Not a slip anywhere either—and just think how tame it all started out!"

She thought about that for a moment. The silver eyes closed slowly; and opened again.

"It's no particular wonder," she remarked, "that Central's picked me for a Five-Agent job—after only five missions! When you get right down to it, you can't beat a Lannai brain!"

The hundred thousand friendly points of light in the vision-tank applauded her silently. Pagadan smiled at them. In the middle of the smile her eyes closed once more—and this time, they stayed closed. Her head began to droop forward.

Then she sat up with a start.

"Hey," she said in drowsy indignation, "what's all this?"

"Sleepy gas," the *Viper's* voice returned. "If you're headed for another job, you're going to sleep all the way to Jeltad. You need your rest."

"That's a whole week!" Pagadan protested. But though she could not remember being transported there, she was in her somno-cabin by then, and flat on her back. Pillows were just being shoved under her head; and lights were going out all over the ship.

"You big, tricky bum!" she muttered. "I'll dismantle your reflexes yet!"

There was no answer to that grim threat; but she couldn't have heard it anyway. A week was due to pass before Zone Agent Pagadan would be permitted to become aware of her surroundings again.

Meanwhile, a dim hum had begun to grow throughout the *Viper's* giant body. Simultaneously, in the darkened and deserted control room, a bright blue spark started climbing steadily up the velocity indicator.

The humming rose suddenly to a howl, thinned out and became inaudible.

The spark stood gleaming steadily then at a point just below the line marked "Emergency."

Space had flattened out before the *Viper*—she was homeward-bound with another mission accomplished.

She began to travel—

THE TRUTH
ABOUT CUSHGAR

THERE WAS, for a time, a good deal of puzzled and uneasy speculation about the methods that had been employed by the Confederacy of Vega in the taming of Cushgar. The disturbing part of it was that nothing really seemed to have happened!

First, the rumor was simply that the Confederacy was preparing to move into Cushgar—and then, suddenly, that it *had* moved in. This aroused surprised but pleased interest in a number of areas bordering the Confederacy. The Thousand Nations and a half-dozen similar organizations quietly flexed their military muscles, and prepared to land in the middle of the Confederacy's back as soon as it became fairly engaged in its ambitious new project. For Cushgar and the Confederacy seemed about as evenly matched as any two powers could possibly be.

But there was no engagement, then. There was not even anything resembling an official surrender. Star system by system, mighty Cushgar was accepting the governors installed by the Confederacy. Meekly, it coughed up what was left of the captive peoples and the loot it had pirated for the past seven centuries. And, very simply and quietly then, under the eyes of a dumfounded galaxy, it settled down and began mending its manners.

Then the rumors began. The wildest of them appeared to have originated in Cushgar itself, among its grim but superstitious inhabitants.

The Thousand Nations and the other rival combines gradually relaxed their various preparations and settled back disappointedly. This certainly wasn't the time to jump! The Confederacy had sneaked something over again; it was all done with by now.

But *what* had they done to Cushgar—and how?

In the Confederacy's Council of Co-ordinators on Vega's planet of Jeltad, the Third Co-ordinator, Chief of the Department of Galactic Zones, was being freely raked over the coals by his eminent colleagues.

They, too, wanted to know about Cushgar; and he wasn't telling.

"Of course, we're not actually accusing you of anything," the Fifth Co-ordinator—Strategics—pointed out. "But you didn't expect to advance the Council's plans by sixty years or thereabouts without arousing a certain amount of curiosity, did you?"

"No, I didn't expect to do that," the Third Co-ordinator admitted.

"Come clean, Train!" said the First. Train was the name by which the Third Co-ordinator was known in this circle. "How did you do it?" Usually they were allies in these little arguments, but the First's curiosity was also rampant.

"Can't tell you!" the Third Co-ordinator said flatly. "I made a report to the College, and they'll dish out to your various departments whatever they ought to get."

He was within his rights in guarding his own department's secrets, and they knew it. As for the College—that was the College of the Pleiades, a metaphysically inclined body which was linked into the affairs of Confederacy government in a manner the College itself presumably could have defined exactly. Nobody else could. However, they were the final arbiters in a case of this kind.

The Council meeting broke up a little later. The Third Co-ordinator left with Bropha, a handsome youngish man who had been listening in, in a liaison capacity for the College.

"Let's go off and have a drink somewhere," Bropha suggested. "I'm curious myself."

The Co-ordinator growled softly. His gray hair was rumpled, and he looked exhausted.

"All right," he said. "I'll tell *you*—"

Bropha's title was President of the College of the Pleiades. That was a good deal less important than it sounded, since he was only the executive scientist in charge of the College's mundane affairs. However, he was also the Third Co-ordinator's close personal friend and had been cleared for secrets of state of any kind whatsoever.

They went off and had their drink.

"You can't blame them too much," Bropha said soothingly. "After all, the conquest of Cushgar has been regarded pretty generally as the Confederacy's principal and most dangerous undertaking in the century immediately ahead. When the Department of Galactic Zones pulls it off suddenly— apparently without preparation or losses—"

"It wasn't without losses," the Co-ordinator said glumly.

"Wasn't it?" said Bropha.

"It cost me," said the Co-ordinator, "the best Zone Agent I ever had—or ever hope to have. Remember Zamm?"

Bropha's handsome face darkened.

Yes, he remembered Zamm! There were even times when he wished he didn't remember her quite so vividly.

But two years would have been much too short an interval in any case to forget the name of the person who had saved his life—

At the time, the discovery that His Excellency the Illustrious Bropha was lost in space had sent a well-concealed ripple of dismay throughout the government of the Confederacy. For Bropha was destined in the Confederacy's plans to become a political figure of the highest possible importance.

Even the Third Co-ordinator's habitual placidity vanished when the information first reached him. But he realized promptly that while a man lost in deep space was almost always lost for good, there were any number of mitigating factors involved in this particular case. The last report on Bropha had been received from his personal yacht, captained by his half brother Greemshard; and that ship was equipped with devices which would have tripped automatic alarms in monitor-stations thousands of light-years apart if it had been suddenly destroyed or incapacitated by any unforeseen accident or space attack.

Since no such alarm was received, the yacht was still functioning undisturbed somewhere, though somebody on board her was keeping her whereabouts a secret.

It all pointed, pretty definitely, at Greemshard!

For its own reasons, the Department of Galactic Zones had assembled a dossier on Bropha's half brother which was hardly less detailed than the information it had available concerning the illustrious scientist himself. It was no secret to its researchers that Greemshard was an ambitious, hard-driving man, who for years had chafed under the fact that the goal of his ambitions was always being reached first and without apparent effort by Bropha. The study of his personality had been quietly extended then to a point where it could be predicted with reasonable accuracy what he would do in any given set of circumstances; and with the department's psychologists busily dissecting the circumstances which surrounded the disappearance of Bropha, it soon became apparent what Greemshard had done and what he intended to do next.

A prompt check by local Zone Agents indicated that none of the powers who would be interested in getting Bropha into their hands had done so as yet, and insured, furthermore, that they could not do so now without leading the Confederacy's searchers directly to him. Which left, as the most important remaining difficulty, the fact that the number of places where the vanished yacht could be kept unobtrusively concealed was enormously large.

The number was a limited one, nevertheless—unless the ship was simply drifting about space somewhere, which was a risk no navigator of Greemshard's experience would be willing to take. And through the facilities of its home offices and laboratories and its roving army of Agents, the Third Department was equipped, as perhaps no other human organization ever had been, to produce an exact chart of all those possible points of concealment and then to check them off in the shortest possible time.

So the Co-ordinator was not in the least surprised when, on the eighth day of the search instigated by the department, a message from Zone Agent Zamman Tarradang-Pok was transferred to him, stating that Bropha had been found, alive and in reasonably good condition, and would be back in his home on Jeltad in another two weeks.

"In a way, though, it's too bad it had to be that space-pixy Zamm who found him!" one of the Co-ordinator's aides remarked.

And to that, after a moment's reflection, the Chief of Galactic Zones agreed.

The moon where Bropha's yacht lay concealed was one of three approximately Earth-sized, ice-encrusted satellites swinging about the sullen glow of a fiery giant-planet.

The robot-ship of Zone Agent Zamman Tarradang-Pok, working along its alloted section of the general search-pattern, flashed in at the moon on a tangent to its orbit, quartered its surface in two sweeping turns and vanished again toward the nearer of the two other satellites.

All in all, that operation was completed in a matter of seconds; but before the ship left, Zone Agent Zamm had disembarked from it in a thirty-foot space-duty skiff—crammed to its skin just now with the kind of equipment required to pull off a miniature invasion-in-force. Whatever sort of camouflaged power station was down there had been shut off the instant it detected her ship's approach. While that didn't necessarily reveal a bad conscience, the momentary pattern of radiations Zamm's instruments had picked up suggested an exact duplicate of the type of engines which powered Bropha's yacht.

So it probably was the yacht, Zamm decided—and it would be hidden just below the moon's frozen surface. She had pinpointed the spot; and on the opposite side of the big satellite the skiff came streaking down into a thin, icy atmosphere.

"You can start hoping that ship was one of those I've been waiting for," Greemshard was remarking meanwhile. "Or else just somebody who isn't interested in us."

He stood in the center of the yacht's control room, staring at Bropha with intense dislike and a touch of fear. A suspicion had begun to grow on Greemshard that with all his cleverness and planning he might have worked himself at last into an impossible situation. None of the dozens of coded messages he had sent out during the past few days had been answered or perhaps even received. It was a little uncanny.

"Whatever happens," he concluded, "they're not getting you back alive!"

Bropha, flattened by gravity shackles to one wall of the room, saw no reason to reply. For the greater part of the past week, he had been floating mentally in some far-off place, from where he detachedly controlled the ceaseless complaints of various abused nerve-endings of his body. His half brother's voice hardly registered. He had begun to review instead, for perhaps the thousandth futile time, the possibilities of the trap into which he had let Greemshard maneuver him. The chances were he would have to pay the usual penalty of stupidity, but it was unlikely that either Greemshard or his confederates would get any benefit out of that.

Bropha was quite familiar—though Greemshard was not —with the peculiar efficiency of the organization headed by his friend, the Third Co-ordinator.

"Do not move, Captain Greemshard!"

That was all that tinkling, brittle voice really said. But it was a moment or so before Bropha grasped the meaning of the words.

He had, he realized, been literally shocked into full consciousness by something that might have been the thin cry of a mindless death as it rose before its victim—a sound that ripped the clogging pain-veils from his thoughts and triggered off an explosion of sheer animal fright. Bropha's brain was a curiously sensitive tool in many ways; it chose to ignore the explicit substance of Zamm's curt warning and, instead, to read in it things like an insatiable hunger, and that ultimate threat. And also, oddly enough, a wailing, bleak despair.

Later on, he would admit readily that in his wracked condition he might have put a good deal more into the voice than was actually there. He would point out, however, that Greemshard, who was not an imaginative man and recklessly brave, seemed to be similarly affected. His half brother, he saw, stood facing him some twenty feet away, with his back to the door that led from the control room into the main body of the yacht; and the expression on his face was one Bropha could never remember afterwards without a feeling of discomfort. There was an assortment of weapons about Greemshard's person and on a desk to one side and within easy reach of him; but for that moment at least he did not move.

Then Bropha's startled gaze shifted beyond Greemshard.

The passage door had disappeared, and a pale-green fire was trickling swiftly from about its frame. He saw Zone Agent Zamm next, standing just beyond the door with a gun in her hand, and several squat, glittering shapes looming up behind her. The shock of almost superstitious fear that had roused him left Bropha in that instant, because he knew at once who and what Zamm was.

At about the same moment, Greemshard made his bid—desperately and with the flashing speed of a big, strong animal in perfect condition.

He flung himself sideways to reach the floor behind the desk, one hand plucking at a gun in his belt; but he was still in mid-leap when some soundless force spun him about and hurled him across the room, almost to Bropha's feet. What was left of Greemshard lay twitching there violently for a few seconds more, and was still. A faint smell of ozone began to spread through the room.

Bropha looked down at the headless body and winced. As children and half-grown boys, he and Greemshard had been the best of friends; and later, he had understood his half brother better than Greemshard ever knew. For a moment at least, the events of the last few days seemed much less important than those years that were past.

Then he looked back at the figure behind the coldly

flaming door frame across the room and stammered: "Thank you, Zone Agent!"

His first glance at Zamm had showed him that she was a Daya-Bal; and up to that moment he would have thought that no branch of humanity was emotionally less suited than they to perform the duties of an Agent of Galactic Zones. But under the circumstances, the person who had effected an entry into that room, in the spectacularly quiet and apparently instantaneous fashion which alone could have saved his life, was not likely to be anything else.

Like a trio of goblin hounds, three different pieces of robotic equipment came variously gliding and floating through the glowing door frame on Zamm's heels, and began to busy themselves gently about a now rather shock-dazed Bropha. His rescuer, he found himself thinking presently, seemed really more bizarre in these surroundings than her mechanical assistants!

Zamm was not in armor but in a fitted spacesuit, so her racial characteristics were unmistakable. By ordinary human standards, the rather small Daya-Bal body was excessively thin and narrow; but Zamm's white face with its pale eyes and thin, straight nose matched it perfectly, and every motion showed the swift, unconscious grace which accounted for some of the fascination her people exerted on their more normally constructed cousins. Bropha, who had spent over a year among the Daya-Bal planets in the Betelgeuse region, and during that time had also come under the spell of what was perhaps the youngest true branch of *Genus Homo*, addressed Zamm, by and by, in her own language.

He noted her smile of quick pleasure and the flash of interest in her eyes, and listened carefully to her reply, which began as an apology for causing irreparable damage to his ship in the process of boarding it. Such responses all seemed disarmingly normal; and he felt unable to recapture the sensations which had awakened him so suddenly when he heard her challenge to Greemshard.

Greemshard's death, too—however he might feel about it personally—was, after all, simply the fate of a criminal who had been misguided enough to resist certain arrest. As

it happened, Bropha never did learn the exact circumstances
under which the four members of Greemshard's little gang,
who were acting as the yacht's crew, had departed this life
just before Zamm appeared at the control room; but it could
be assumed that the situation there had been a somewhat
similar one.

His explanations, however, completely failed to satisfy
him—because he knew the Daya-Bals.

He spent most of the two weeks required for the return
trip to Jeltad in a bed under robotic treatment.

The physical damage his misadventure had cost him wasn't
too serious, but it had to be repaired promptly; and such
first-aid patchwork usually involved keeping a human brain
anaesthetized to the point of complete unconsciousness. But
Bropha's level of mind-training permitted him to by-pass that
particular effect, and to remain as aware of his surroundings
as he chose to be; and he remained much more aware of
them than Zamman Tarradang-Pok or her robots appeared
to realize.

To the average bedridden traveler, that endless drive on a
silent ship through the unreal-seeming voids of the overspeed
might have seemed monotonous to the point of dreary bore-
dom. Bropha—alert, wondering and reflecting—soon gained
a different impression of it. Little enough was actually hap-
pening; but even the slightest events here seemed weighted
to him with some abnormal dark significance of their own.
It was almost, he thought, as if he were catching an occasional whispered line or two of some grim drama—the ac-
tors of which moved constantly all about him but were very
careful to stay out of his sight!

One day, finally, his watching was briefly rewarded; though
what he observed left him, if anything, more puzzled than
before. But afterwards, he found that a faint echo of the
chill Zamm's voice first aroused in him had returned. In
his mind, it now accompanied the slight shape which came
occasionally through the shadowed passage before his cabin
and, much more rarely, paused there quietly to look in on
him.

Simultaneously, he discovered that a sense of something

depressing and frightening had crept into his concept of this stupendously powered ship of Zamm's, with its electronic mentality through which sensations and reflexes flashed in a ceaseless billionfold shift of balances, over circuits and with meanings to which nothing remotely like a parallel existed in any human brain. Its racing drive through apparent nothingness, at speeds which no longer could be related mentally to actual motion, was like the expression of some fixed, nightmarish purpose which Bropha's presence had not changed in any way. For the moment, he was merely being carried along in the fringe of the nightmare—soon he would be expelled from it.

And then that somehow terrible unit, the woman of a race which mankind had long regarded as if they were creatures of some galactic Elfland—beings a little wiser, gentler, a little farther from the brute than their human brothers—and her train of attendant robots, of which there seemed to be a multi-shaped, grotesque insect-swarm about the ship, and finally the titanic, man-made monster that carried them all, would go rushing off again on their ceaseless, frightening search.

For what?

Without being able to give himself a really good reason for it even now, Bropha was, in brief, profoundly disturbed.

But one day he came walking up into the control room, completely healed again, though still a little uncertain in his stride and more than a little dissatisfied in his thoughts. Vega was now some twenty-five light-years away in space; but in the foreshortening magic of the ship's vision tank, its dazzling, blue-white brilliance floated like a three-inch fire-jewel before them. A few hours later, great Jeltad itself swam suddenly below with its wind-swept blues and greens and snowy poles—to the eyes of the two watchers on the ship much more like the historical Earth-home of both their races than the functional, tunneled hornet-hive that Terra was nowadays.

So Bropha came home. Being Bropha, his return was celebrated as a planetary event that night, centered about a flamboyant festival at his fine house overlooking the tall, gray towers of Government Center. Being also the Bropha who could not leave any human problem unsettled, once it came to his attention, he tried to make sure that the festival would be attended both by his rescuer and by her boss—his old friend, the Third Co-ordinator of the Vegan Confederacy.

However, only one of them appeared.

"To tell you the truth," Bropha remarked, "I didn't expect her to show up. And to tell you the truth again, I feel almost relieved, now that she didn't." He nodded down at the thronged and musical garden stretches below the gallery in which they sat. "I can't imagine Zamm in a setting like that!"

The Co-ordinator looked. "No," he agreed thoughtfully; "Zamm wouldn't fit in."

"It would be," said Bropha, rather more dramatically than was customary for him, "like seeing some fever-dream moving about in your everyday life—it wouldn't do!"

"So you want to talk about her," the Co-ordinator said; and Bropha realized suddenly that his friend looked soberly amused.

"I do," he admitted. "In fact, it's necessary! That Agent of yours made me extremely uneasy."

The Co-ordinator nodded.

"It hasn't anything to do," Bropha went on, "with the fact of her immense personal attractiveness. After all, that's an almost uniform quality of her race. I've sometimes thought that racial quality of the Daya-Bals might be strong enough to have diverted our sufficiently confused standards of such abstractions as beauty and perfection into entirely new channels—if their people happened to be spread out among our A-Class civilizations."

The Co-ordinator laughed. "It just might be, at that! Perhaps it's fortunate for us they've lost the urges of migrating and dominating the widest possible range of surroundings."

Bropha didn't agree.

"If they hadn't lost them," he said, "they'd be something other than they are—probably something a good deal less formidable. As it is, they've concentrated on themselves. I've heard them described as metaphysicists and artists. But those are our terms. Personally I think the Daya-Bals understand such terms in a way we don't. While I was living among them, anyway, I had a constant suspicion that they moved habitually in dimensions of mental reality I didn't know of as yet—"

He stopped and hauled himself back.

"You were going to speak of Zamm," his friend reminded him.

"Well, in a way I *am* speaking of her!" Bropha said slowly. "Obviously, the mere fact that a Daya-Bal is working for you, for the Department of Galactic Zones—and operating one of those really hellish robot ships of yours—is a flat contradiction to everything we know about them. Or think we know! A fallen angel would seem much less of a paradox. And there was the manner in which she killed Greemshard—"

The Co-ordinator raised a bushy gray eyebrow.

"Naturally," Bropha assured him, "I'm not blaming her for Greemshard's death. Under the circumstances, that had become unavoidable, in any case. But Zamm killed him"— he was selecting his words carefully now—"as if she were under some inescapable compulsion to do it. I don't know how else to describe the action."

He waited, but Zamm's boss offered no comment.

"There were two other incidents," Bropha continued, "on our way back here. The first was on the same day that we took off from that chunk of ice of a moon. We chased something. I didn't see what it was and I didn't ask her. There was a little maneuvering and a fairly long, straight run, about two minutes. We got hit by something heavy enough to slow us; and then the ship's automatics went off. That was all. Whatever it was, it was finished."

"It was finished, all right!" the Co-ordinator stated. "That was a Shaggar ship. They seem to be migrating through that section. Zamm reported the incident, and as I was following your return with interest, I heard of it directly."

"I'm not questioning the ethics of your Agent's work, you know," Bropha said after a pause. "Having seen something of what the Shaggar will do to anybody who can't outfight them, I also realize that killing them, in particular, is in a class with destroying a plague virus. No, the point is simply that I saw Zamm's face immediately afterwards. She came past my cabin and looked in at me for a moment. I don't believe she actually saw me! Her eyes looked blind. And her face had no more expression than a white stone—"

He added doubtfully, "And that's not right either! Because at the same time I had the very clear impression that she was staring past me at something. I remember thinking that she hated whatever she saw there with an intensity no sane being should feel against anything." He paused again. "You know now what I'm trying to say?"

"It's fairly obvious," the Co-ordinator replied judicially, "that you believe one of my Agents, at least, is a maniac."

"It sounds thoroughly ungrateful to me," Bropha nodded, "but that's about it—except, of course, that I don't actually believe it! However, for the sake of my own peace of mind, I'd be obliged if you'd take the trouble to look up the facts on Zone Agent Zamm and let me know what the correct explanation is."

It was the Co-ordinator who hesitated now.

"She's a killer, certainly," he said at last. He smiled faintly. "In fact, Bropha, you've been granted the distinction of being rescued by what is quite probably the grand champion killer of the department. Zamm's a Peripheral Agent—roving commission you might call it. No fixed zone of operations. When she runs out of work, she calls in to Central and has them lay out a pattern of whatever foci of disturbance there are in the areas she's headed for. She checks in here at Jeltad about once a year to have her ship equipped with any worthwhile innovations Lab's cooked up in the interval."

He reflected a moment. "I don't know," he said, "whether you were in a condition to notice much about that ship of hers?"

"Not much," Bropha admitted. "I remember, when she called it back to pick us up, it seemed bulkier than most Agent ships I'd seen—a big, dull-black spheroid mostly. I saw very little of its interior. Why?"

"As an Agent ship, it's our ultimate development in self-containment," the Co-ordinator said. "In that particular type, camouflage and inconspicuousness are largely sacrificed to other advantages. Self-repair's one of them; it could very nearly duplicate itself in case of need. Those are the peripheral ships—almost perpetual travelers. The Agents who direct them prowl along the fringes of our civilizations and deal with whatever needs to be dealt with there before it gets close enough to cause serious trouble."

"I understand the need for such Agents," Bropha said slowly. "I should think, however, that they would be selected for such work with particular care."

"They are," said the Co-ordinator.

"Then supposing," said Bropha, "that another people, like the Daya-Bals—who are experts in other branches of robotics—came into possession of such a ship. They could duplicate it eventually?"

"After some fifty years of study, they could," the Co-ordinator agreed. "It wouldn't worry us much since we expect to be studying hard ourselves throughout any given fifty years of history. Actually, of course, we have a theory that our Agents are psychologically incapable of giving away departmental secrets in a manner that could cause us harm."

"I know," said Bropha. "That's why I was surprised to discover that there are . . . or were . . . two other Daya-Bals on Zamm's ship."

For the first time, the Co-ordinator looked a little startled. "What made you think so?"

"I heard them talking," Bropha said, "on various occasions, though I didn't make out what they said. And finally I saw them—they came past my door, following Zamm." He paused. "I was under drugs at the time," he admitted, "and under treatment generally. But I can assure you that those incidents were not hallucinations."

"I didn't think they were," said the Co-ordinator. "Is that why you're trying to check on Zamm's motivations?"

Bropha hesitated. "It's one of the reasons."

The Co-ordinator nodded. "Fifteen years ago, Zamm lost her husband and child in a space attack on a Daya-Bal liner. There were three survivors—Zamm was one—but

they'd been unconscious through most of the action and
could give no description of the attackers. The bodies of
most of the other passengers and of the crew were identified,
but about fifty remained unaccounted for. Zamm's husband
and child were among that number. She believes they were
taken along alive by the unknown beings that wrecked and
looted the ship."

"That's not so unreasonable!" Bropha said. But he looked
rather shaken, suddenly.

"No," agreed the Co-ordinator. "Under the circumstances,
though, it's extremely unreasonable of her to expect to find
them again. You might say that Zamm is under a delusion
in that she believes she will be able to beat probability at
such outrageous odds. But that's the extent of her 'insanity'
—according to our psychologists."

Bropha started to speak, but then shook his head.

"So it's not too hard to understand that Zamm hates the
things she hunts," the Co-ordinator pointed out. "In her
eyes, they must be much the same as the things that took her
family from her—they might even, by coincidence, be those
very things themselves!"

"But that doesn't—" Bropha began again.

"And her delusion appears to have blinded her neither to
the difficulties of the task nor to the methods most likely to
overcome them," the Co-ordinator continued blandly. "A
few years after her loss, she reduced the odds against her at
one stroke to the lowest practical level by coming to work
for us. In effect, that put the Department of Galactic Zones
permanently on the job of helping her in her search! For the
past dozen years, any trace of a Daya-Bal any of our opera-
tives has discovered outside of the Betelgeuse Zone has
been reported to Zamm in a matter of hours. Now, those
two you saw on her ship—can you describe them?"

"It was dark in the passage," Bropha said hesitantly. He
was a little pale now. "However, I couldn't be mistaken! It
was a man and a boy."

The Co-ordinator was silent for a moment.

"I thought it would be that," he admitted. "Well, it's an
unpleasant notion to our way of thinking, I grant you—even
a somewhat nightmarish one. There's a flavor of necroman-

cy. However, you can see it's obviously not a matter that involves any question of Zamm's loyalty. As you say, the Daya-Bals are very clever in robotics. And she was a neurosurgeon before she came to us. Those were just two marionettes, Brophaǃ"

He stood up. "Shall we rejoin your party, now?"

Bropha had come to his feet, too. "And you still say she isn't insane?" he cried.

The Co-ordinator spread his hands. "So far as I can see, your experience offers no contradictory proofǃ So I shall simply continue to rely on the department's psychologists. You know their verdict: that whatever our Agents may do, their judgment will be almost as nearly infallible as it is possible for highly-trained human-type intelligences to become. And, further, that no matter how widely their motivations may vary, they will not vary ever to the extent of being unacceptable to the department."

Three days out in space by now, Zone Agent Zamm was rapidly approaching the point at which she had first swerved aside to join the search for Bropha.

She was traveling fast—a great deal faster than she had done while taking her damaged and politically valuable passenger home. With him on board she'd felt obliged to loiter, since the department did not recommend top velocities when some immediate emergency wasn't impending. Only vessels of the truly titanic bulk of Vega's Giant Rangers could navigate with apparent safety at such speeds; while to smaller ships things were likely to happen—resulting usually in sudden and traceless disappearances which had been the subject of much unsatisfactory theorizing in Department Lab and similar scientific centers throughout civilization. But Zamm was impatient both with the numbing, senseless vastness of space and with its less open dangers. Let it snap at her from ambush if it likedǃ It always missed.

"Want a hot-spot chart on this line I'm following, for a week's cruising range," she informed the ship's telepath transmitter; and her request was repeated promptly in Galactic Zones Central on the now faraway planet of Jeltad.

Almost as promptly, a three-dimensional star-map swam

into view on the transmitter-screen before Zamm. She studied it thoughtfully.

The green dot in the center indicated her position. Visually, it coincided with the fringe of a group of short crimson dashes denoting the estimated present position of the migrating Shaggar ships she had contacted briefly and reported on her run to Jeltad. A cloud of white light far ahead was a civilized star cluster. Here and there within that cluster, and scattered also around the periphery of the chart, some dozens of near-microscopic sun-systems stood circled in lines of deep red. Enclosing the red circles appeared others: orange, purple, green—indicating the more specific nature of the emergency.

Zamm stabbed a pointer at three systems marked thus as focal points of trouble inviting a Zone Agent's attention, near the far left of the chart.

"Going to try to pick up the Shaggar drift again," she announced. "If we find it, we ought to be somewhere up in that area before we're done with them. Get me the particulars on what's wrong around there, and home it out to me. That's all—"

She switched off the transmitter. The star-map vanished and a soft, clear light filled the room. Zamm rubbed a thin, long hand over her forearm and blinked pale eyes at the light. "How about a snack?" she asked.

A food tray slid out of the wall to a side table of the big desk, its containers variously iced or steaming.

She ate slowly and lightly, mentally organizing the period of time ahead. Only for a few weeks—once she had laid out plans for a year or more—so and so many planets to investigate—such and such a field to cover! But the hugeness of the task had gradually overwhelmed her will to major planning. Now she moved about in briefer spurts, not aimlessly but diverted toward new areas constantly by hunches, sudden impulses and hopes—careful only not to retrace her tracks any more than could be avoided.

But she was beaten, she knew. She'd never find them! Neither would any of the thousands and thousands of people she'd set watching and looking for traces of them. The Universe that had taken them was the winner.

She glanced over at the black, cold face that filled the whole of her ship's vision tank, its million glittering eyes mocking her.

"Stupid thing—grinning!" she whispered, hating it tiredly. She got up and started moving restlessly about the big room.

Black Face out there was her enemy! She could hurt it a little, but not much. Not enough to count. It was so big it only had to wait. For centuries; for thousands, for tens of thousands and hundreds of thousands of years. Waiting while life built up somewhere, warm and brave and frail and hopeful—then it came suddenly with its flow of cold foulness to end it again! With some ravaging, savage destruction from outside, like the Shaggar; or more subtly with a dark pulse that slowly poisoned the mind of a race. Or it might be even only a single intelligent brain in which the cold death pattern grew till it burst out suddenly to engulf a nation, a planet—There was simply no end to the number and kinds of weapons the Universe had against life!

Zamm had stopped her pacing. She stood looking down at a big couch in the center of the room.

"You shouldn't try mind-search now, Zamm!" The voice of the gigantic robot that was the ship came, almost anxiously, into the room. "You've been under severe emotional tensions throughout the past weeks!"

"I know," she murmured. "Glad they got him back though —nice people; nice guy! We worried him, I think—" She kicked the side of the couch reflectively with the tip of one soft boot. "Those tensions might help, you know! Send the doll out and we'll see."

"The big one?" the voice inquired.

"No!" said Zamm with a sort of terror. "Can't stand to look at him when I'm all alone. No, the little one—"

Somewhere in the ship a door opened and closed. After a few seconds, footsteps came running, lightly, swiftly. A small shape scampered into the room, stopped, glanced about with bright sharp eyes, saw Zamm and ran to her.

She opened her arms and swept up the shape as it flung itself at her laughing.

"What an artist made those masks!" she said wonderingly, her fingertips tracing over a cheek of the face that was very like her own and yet different. "You couldn't tell by just touching—!" She smiled down at the shape cradled in her arms. "Fifteen years! Be a bigger boy now—but not too much. We don't shoot up quick like those old A-Class humans, do we? But for that, we grow up smarter. Don't we?"

The shape chuckled amiable agreement. Zamm blinked at it, half-smiling but alert, as if listening to something within herself. The dolls had very little in common with her working robots; they were designed to be visual hypnotics, compelling and dangerous agents that could permanently distort the fabric of sanity. Those of her people who had helped her in their design had done it reluctantly, though they understood the value of such devices for one who went searching in memory for what she had lost in time. With almost clinical detachment, she watched herself being drawn under the familiar compulsion that seemed to combine past and present, illusion and reality, until something stormy and cold washed suddenly through her face, slackening its features. Then she closed her eyes for a moment, and set the shape carefully back on its feet on the floor.

"Run along, little boy!" she told it absently, her face taut and blank once more. "Back to your place! Mother's busy."

Its gurgle of laughter merged into a receding rush of footsteps. Presently a door clicked shut again, somewhere.

Zamm went slowly to the couch and lay down on it, flat on her back, arms over her head.

"We'll try mind-search now!" she said.

The robot made no comment. A half-score glassy tentacles came out from under the couch and began to fasten themselves here and there over Zamm's body, coiled about her skull and glued flaring tips to her temples.

"I'm set," she said. "Let it go!"

A faint humming rose from the wall. Her body stiffened suddenly, went rigid, and then relaxed completely.

There had been a brief awareness of cold, rushing inwards from all sides. But almost instantly, it reached and chilled the nerve-linkages at which it was directed.

Incoming sensation ceased with that, abruptly. Zamm's

brain swam alone, released, its consciousness diffused momentarily over an infinity of the what-had-been, the time-past—but also over deceptively similar infinities of the might-have-been, the never-was. Those swirling universes of events and symbols would crystallize now, obediently but not necessarily truthfully, into whatever pattern consciousness chose to impress on them.

The brain could fool itself there! But it had an ally who wouldn't be tricked.

It ordered:

"Back to just before it began!"

Swarm after swarm of neurons woke suddenly to the spreading advance of the robot's stimulating, probing forces through their pathways. Million-factored time-past events formed briefly, were discarded and combined anew. At last, familiar images began to flick up and reel away within the brain. Remembered sound crashed; remembered warmth swept in—pain, cold, touch, rest.

Hate, love, terror—possession, loss.

"We're there! Where it began."

There was the darkened cabin on the doomed spaceliner; only a small pool of amber light glowed against one tapestried wall. Distant and faint came the quivering of gigantic engines.

"They hadn't quite worked the shake out of them, those days," Zamm's brain remembered.

She lay on the cabin's big bed, lazing, content, half asleep on her side, blinking at the amber glow. She'd been first to take note of the rest period's arrival and come back to the cabin. As usual.

". . . . used to love to sleep, those days!"

Her menfolk were still playing around somewhere in the vacation ship's variously and beautifully equipped playrooms. The big one and the little one—should be getting more rest, both of them! What's a vacation for, otherwise?

Zamm was beginning to wonder idly just where they'd gone to loiter this time, when the amber light flickered twice—

"It's begun!"

Roar of sound, flash of light! Then the blaring attack-alarm from the cabin's communicator was cut short; and a body went flip-flopping crazily about the room like an experimental animal speared by an electric current. Everywhere, the liner's injured artificial gravs were breaking circuits, reforming instantly, breaking at other points; and reforming again. And holding at last, locked into a new, emergency-created pattern.

But in the cabin was darkness and unconsciousness, while over the fifteen years, for the two-thousandth time, Zamm's brain strained and tore for the one look out, the one identifiable sound—perhaps even a touch. A fraction of a second might be all she'd need!

And it had lasted two hours, that period! For two hours, *they* swarmed about the ship they had murdered, looting, despoiling, dragging away the ones still alive and not too badly hurt. They must have come into the cabin more than once, prowled about it, stared at her, touched her. Gone on—

But—nothing.

Full consciousness emerged suddenly at the same point as always. Then the body went crawling and scrambling up the tilted flat of a floor, tilted irrevocably now in the new gravitational pattern the stricken liner had achieved for its rigor mortis. Broken bone in lower right arm, right ankle flapping loosely—like the splintered cabin door overhead, that flapped from what was now one edge of a tilted ceiling! From somewhere within the ship came the steady roar of atomic fires; and then sudden sounds like the yelping of animals, rising into long shrieks.

"The ray-burned ones!" gasped Zamm, as the clambering body stiffened in horror, unmoving, listening. "But those weren't mine!" she screamed. "I checked them all!" She caught herself. "Wait—I'll have to go through that period again."

"You can't do that twice!" the robot's voice said. "Not now. Not that part!"

"Well—" It was right, of course. It usually was. "Get on with the sequence then!"

"Even that's too dangerous. You're nearly exhausted, Zamm!"

But the body reached for the edge of the door, hung on with the good arm, kicked with both legs and wriggled over awkwardly into a bright-lit corridor, slanted upward at a nightmarish angle. Other bodies lay there, in tumbled piles, not moving.

"If I hadn't stopped to check those—If I'd looked up sooner—just a few seconds sooner!"

One by one, the lost seconds passed away as always, and then the body suddenly looked up. A bright glare filled the upper end of the tilted corridor. Something had moved within that glare of light—had just crossed the corridor and was disappearing again down another hallway that angled off it, slanting downwards. The light followed the moving shape like a personal shadow and vanished behind it.

"Working in individual light-barriers, making a last check before they left," murmured Zamm, while the body crawled and hobbled toward the point where the light had been, screaming with terror, rage, question and despair.

"If I'd looked up that moment sooner, I'd have seen what they were like, even in space armor—human or what. I'd have *seen!*"

She found herself staring up at the ceiling of her ship's control room, muttering the worn old words.

She stirred stiffly but made no attempt to sit up.

"Nearly went out here," she said tonelessly.

"That was dangerous, Zamm," said the robot-voice. "I warned you."

"No harm done!" she said. "Next time, we'll just work the unconscious period through all by itself."

She lay quiet, her mouth bitter. Somewhere in memory, as somewhere in space, were points where she might pick up their trail. Things she had experienced in those hours but not consciously remembered. Scattered groups of cells within the bony box that enclosed her brain still held them locked.

Statistically, it couldn't happen that she would ever flood any specific group of cells with the impulse-pattern that re-vived those specific flickers of memory. Statistically, it would be a whole lot easier even to pick the one sun-system and planet where they might be out of the numberless fiery cells that were the galaxy's body!

But she was still learning! One way or the other, she was going to do it. Find them—

Zamm lay there, staring upwards, bitter and unbelieving.

"What is it?" she asked suddenly.

"Company!" the robot said.

They were a long, long distance away, moving at many times the speed of light. In the vision tank, they seemed to glide past unhurriedly almost within shouting range of the ship. One, two, three, four—

Four clouds of diffused radiance, like great, luminous jellyfish pulsing down an indetectable current of space. Migrating Shaggar ships behind their camouflaging screens. They had spotted her, of course, but like most of the older forms of space life they had learned to be careful about strange ships that did not flee from them at once. They were waiting to see her next move.

"Confirm position and direction of the drift for Central first!" Zamm said. Despair and rage were still bleak in her eyes, but her long, tapered fingers slid swiftly and surely above and about the armament banks of the control desk. Not touching anything just yet; only checking.

"Two of these are nearly in line," the robot reported.

"Five in all!" sniffed Zamm. "One more could make it a fight. Parallel course, and swing round once to make them bunch up—"

A minute or so later, they flashed across the Shaggars' path, at point-blank range ahead of them. The nebular screens vanished suddenly, and five deep-bellied, dark ships became visible instead. Light and energy boiled abruptly all about Zamm's black globe—before, behind. It missed.

"Spot any more, this side?"

"Four more are approaching—barely detectable! They may have been called by this group."

"Good enough! We'll take them next." Zamm waited as the ship completed its swing and drove into line behind her quarry. They were beyond any weapon-reach by then,

ut space far ahead was being churned into a long whirl-
ool of flame. At the whirlpool's core, the five Shaggar ships,
etreating at speed, had drawn close together and were
irowing back everything they had.

"Instructions?" the robot-voice murmured.

"Contact range— Move in!"

Up the long cone of flame, the ship sprang at the five.
amm's hands soared, spread and high, above the arma-
ient banks—thin, curved, white claws of hate! Those seem-
ig to swim down toward her now, turning and shifting
lowly within their fire-veils, were not the faceless, more
r less humanlike ones she sought. But they were marked
*ith the same red brand: brand of the butchers, looters,
espoilers—of all the death-thoughts drifting and writhing
hrough the great stupid carnivore mind of the Universe—

At point-blank range, a spectral brilliance clung and ham-
iered at her ship and fell away. At half-range, the ship
huddered and slowed like a beast plowing through a mud-
iole and out. At one-quarter, space turned to solid, jarring
ire for seconds at a time.

Zamm's hands flashed.

"NOW—"

A power ravened ahead of them then like the bellow-
ig of a sun. Behind it, hardly slower, all defenses cut
nd every weapon blaring its specific ultimate of destruc-
ion, the ship came screaming the hate of Zamm.

Two years—

The king-shark was bothering Zamm! It hung around
ome subspace usually where she couldn't hope to trace it.

It was a big ship, fast and smart and tricky. It had
reapons and powers of which she knew nothing. She
ouldn't even guess whether it realized she was on its tail
r not. Probably, it didn't.

Its field of operations was wide enough so that its regularly
paced schedule of kills didn't actually disrupt traffic there
r scare it away. A certain percentage of losses had to
e taken for granted in interstellar commerce. The chief
ifference seemed to be that in this area the losses all went
) the king-shark.

Zamm circled after it, trying to calculate its next points of appearance. A dozen times she didn't miss it by much; but its gutted kills were still all she got.

It took no avoidable chances. It picked its prey and came boiling up into space beside it—or among it, if it was a small convoy—and did its work. It didn't bother with prisoners, so the work was soon done. In an hour everything was over. The dead hulks with their dead crews and dead passengers went drifting away for Zamm to find. The king-shark was gone again.

Disgusted, Zamm gave up trying to outguess it. She went off instead and bought herself a freighter.

The one she selected was an expensive, handsome ship, and she loaded it up with a fortune. She wanted no gilded hook for the king-shark; she'd feed it solid gold! There were a dozen fortunes lying around her globe, in salvaged cash and whatnot from previous jobs. She'd use it up as she needed it or else drop it off at Jeltad the next time she went back. Nobody kept accounts on that sort of stuff.

Her freighter was all ready to start.

"Now I need a nice pirate!" mused Zamm.

She went out and caught herself one. It had an eighteen-man crew, and that was just right for the freighter. She checked over their memories first, looking for the one thing she wanted. It wasn't there. A lot of other things were, but it had been a long time since that kind of investigation made her feel particularly sick.

"Anyone lives through it, I'll let him go!" she promised, cold-eyed. She would, and they knew it. They were small fry; let somebody else grab them up if they wanted them badly enough!

At a good, fast, nervous pace, the freighter and its crew crossed what was currently the most promising section of the king-shark's area—Zamm's black globe sliding and shifting and dancing about its bait at the farthest possible range that would still permit it to pounce.

By and by, the freighter came back on another route and passed through the area again. It was nearing the end of the fourth pass when the king-shark surfaced into space

beside it and struck. In that instant, the freighter's crew
died; and Zamm pounced.

It wasn't just contact range; it was contact. Alloy hide
to alloy hide, Zamm's round black leech clung to the king-
shark's flank, their protective screens fused into a single use-
less mass about them. It didn't matter at what point the
leech started to bite; there weren't any weak ones. Nor
were there any strong enough to stop its cutter-beam at a
four-foot range.

It was only a question of whether they could bring up
something in eighty seconds that would blast out the leech's
guts as the wall between them vanished.

They couldn't, it seemed. Zamm and her goblin crew
of robots went into the king-shark in a glittering wave.

"Just mess up their gravs!" said Zamm. "They don't
carry prisoners. There'll be some in suits, but we'll handle
them."

In messed-up rows, the robots laid out the living and
the nearly dead about the king-shark's passages and rooms.

"From Cushgar!" said Zamm surprised. "They're prowling a long way from home!"

She knew them by their looks. The ancestors of the
king-shark's one hundred and fourteen crewmen had also
once breathed the air of Terra. They had gone off elsewhere and mutated variously then; and, like the Daya-Bals,
the strongest surviving mutant strains eventually had blended
and grown again to be a new race.

Not a handsome one, by Zamm's standards! Short and
squat and hairy, and enormously muscled. The spines of
their neck and back vertebrae stuck out through their skins
in horny spikes, like the ridge on a turtle's shell. But she'd
seen worse-looking in the human line; and she wasn't judg-
ing a beauty contest.

A robot stalked briskly along the rows like a hunting
wasp, pausing to plunge a fine needle into the neck of each
of the people from Cushgar, just beneath the fourth verte-
bral spike. Zamm and a robot that had loafed till now
picked out the ones that seemed damaged worst, settled
down beside each in turn and began their questioning.

Some time passed—four, five hours—finally six. Then Zamm and her robots came back to her ship. The leech sealed its egress port, unclamped and took off. The king-shark's huge, dark hulk went drifting along through space. There was no one alive on it now. Fifteen minutes later, a light suddenly flared from it, and it vanished.

Zamm sat white-faced and silent at her desk for a much longer time than that.

"The dolls," she said finally, aloud.

"Yes?" said the big robot-voice.

"Destroy them," said Zamm. She reached out and switched on the telepath transmitter. "And get me a line through to Jeltad. The Co-ordinator—"

There was no reply, and no sound came from within the ship. She lit up some star-globes and began calculating from them. The calculations didn't take long. Then she sat still again for a while, staring into the luminous green, slowly swirling haze that filled the transmitter screen.

A shape and a face began forming in it at last; and a voice pronounced her name questioningly.

"They're in Cushgar!" said Zamm, the words running out in a brittle, tinkling rush. "I know the planet and the place. I saw them the way *it* saw them—the boy's getting pretty big. It's a gray house at a sort of big hospital. Seventeen years they've been working there! Seventeen years, working for them!" Her face was grisly with hate.

The Co-ordinator waited till the words had all run out. He looked rather sick.

"You can't go there alone!" he said.

"How else!" Zamm said surprised. "Who'd be going with me there? But I've got to take the ship. I wanted to tell you."

The Co-ordinator shook his head.

"You bought the ship with your second mission! But you can't go there alone, Zamm. You'll be passing near enough to Jeltad on your way there, anyway. Stop in, and we'll think of something!"

"You can't help me," Zamm told him bluntly. "You can't mission anybody into Cushgar. You lost every Agent you ever sent there. You try a Fleet squadron, and it's war. Thousand Nations would jump you the day after!"

"There's always another way," the Co-ordinator said. He paused a moment, looking for that other way. "You stay near your transmitter anyhow! I'll call you as soon as we can arrange some reasonable method—"

"No," said Zamm. "I can't take any more calls either—I just got off a long run. I'm hitting Deep Rest now till we make the first hostile contact. I've only got one try, and I've got to give it everything. There's no other way," she added, "and there aren't any reasonable methods. I thought it all out. But thanks for the ship!"

The Co-ordinator located the man called Snoops over a headquarters' communicator and spoke to him briefly.

Snoops swore softly.

"She's got other friends who would want to be told," the Co-ordinator concluded. "I'm leaving that to you."

"You would," said Snoops. "You going to be in your office? I might need some authority!"

"You don't need authority," the Co-ordinator said, "and I just started on a fishing trip. I've had a vacation coming these last eight years—I'm going to take it."

Snoops scowled unpleasantly at the dead communicator. He had no official position in the department. He had a long suite of offices and a laboratory, however. His business was to know everything about everybody, as he usually did.

He scratched his bearded chin and gave the communicator's tabs a few vindictive punches. It clicked back questioningly.

"Want a location check on forty-two thousand and a couple of hundred names!" Snoops said. "Get busy!"

The communicator groaned.

Snoops ignored it. He was stabbing at a telepath transmitter.

"Hi, Ferd!" he said presently.

"Almighty sakes, Snoops," said Ferdinand the Finger. "Don't unload anything new on me now! I'm right in the middle—"

"Zamm's found out about her kin," said Snoops. "They're in Cushgar! She's gone after them."

Zone Agent Ferdinand swore. His lean, nervous fingers worked at the knot of a huge scarlet butterfly cravat. He was a race tout at the moment—a remarkably good one.

"Where'd she contact from?" he inquired.

Snoops told him.

"That's right on my doorstep," said Ferdinand.

"So I called you first," Snoops said. "But you can't contact her. She's traveling Deep Rest."

"Is, huh? What's Bent say?" asked Ferdinand.

"Bent isn't talking—he went fishing. Hold on there!" Snoops added hastily. "I wasn't done!"

"Thanks a lot for calling, Snoops," Ferdinand said with his hand on the transmitter switch. "But I'm right in the middle—"

"You're in the middle of the Agent-list of that cluster," Snoops informed him. "I just unloaded it on you!"

"That'll take me hours!" Ferdinand howled. "You can't—"

"Just parcel it out," Snoops said coldly. "You're the executive type, aren't you? You can do it while you're traveling. I'm busy!"

He cut off Ferdinand the Finger.

"How you coming?" he asked the communicator.

"That's going to be over eighteen thousand to locate!" the communicator grumbled.

"Locate 'em," said Snoops. He was punching the transmitter again. When you want to get in touch with even just the key-group of the Third Department's forty-two thousand and some Zone Agents, you had to keep on punching!

"Hi, Senator!"

If anyone was amusing himself that week by collecting reports of extraordinary events, with the emphasis on mysterious disappearances, he ran into a richer harvest than usual.

It caused a quite exceptional stir, of course, when Senator Thartwith excused himself in the middle of a press interview, stepped into the next office to take an urgent personal call, and failed to reappear. For the senator was a prominent public figure—the Leader of the Opposition in the Thousand Nations. He had closed the door behind him; but his celebrated sonorous voice was heard raised in apparent expostulation for about a minute thereafter. Then all became still.

Half an hour passed before an investigation was risked. It disclosed, by and by, that the senator had quite vanished!

He stayed vanished for a remarkable length of time. In a welter of dark suspicions, the Thousand Nations edged close to civil war.

Of only planetary interest, though far more spectacular, was the sudden ascension of the Goddess Loppos of Amuth in her chariot drawn by two mystical beasts, just as the conclusion of the Annual Temple Ceremony of Amuth began. A few moments before the event, the Goddess was noted to frown, and her lips appeared to move in a series of brisk, celestial imprecations. Then the chariot shot upwards; and a terrible flash of light was observed in the sky a short while later. Amuth bestrewed its head with ashes and mourned for a month until Loppos reappeared.

Mostly, however, these freakish occurrences involved personalities of no importance and so caused no more than a splash of local disturbance. As when Grandma Wannattel quietly unhitched the rhinocerine pony from her patent-medicine trailer and gave the huge but patient animal to little Grimp to tend—"Until I come back." Nothing would have been made of that incident at all—police and people were always bothering poor Grandma Wannattel and making her move on—if Grimp had not glanced back, just as he got home with the pony, and observed Grandma's big trailer soaring quietly over a hillside and on into the sunset. Little Grimp caught it good for that whopper!

In fact, remarkable as the reports might have seemed to a student of such matters, the visible flow of history was at all affected by only one of them. That was the unfortunate case of Dreem, dread Tyrant of the twenty-two Heebelant Systems:

". . . and me all set to be assassinated by the Freedom Party three nights from now!" roared Dreem. "Take two years to needle the chicken livered bunch up to it again!"

"Suit yourself, chum!" murmured the transmitter above his bed.

"That I will," the despot grumbled, groping about for his slippers. "You just bet your life I will!"

"We should be coming within instrument-detection of the van of the ghost fleet almost immediately!" the adjutant of the Metag of Cushgar reported.

"Don't use that term again!" the potentate said coldly. "It's had a very bad effect on morale. If I find it in another official communication, there'll be a few heads lifted from their neck-spines. Call them 'the invaders.' "

The adjutant muttered apologies.

"How many invaders are now estimated in that first group?" the Metag inquired.

"Just a few thousand, sir," the adjutant said. "The reports, of course, remain very—vague! The main body seems to be still about twelve light-years behind. The latest reports indicate approximately thirty thousand there."

The Metag grunted. "We should be just able to intercept that main bunch with the *Glant* then!" he said. "If they keep to their course, that is. It's high time to end this farce!"

"They don't appear to have swerved from their course to avoid interception yet," the adjutant ventured.

"They haven't met the *Glant* yet, either!" the Metag returned grinning.

He was looking forward to that meeting. His flagship, *Glant,* the spindle-shaped giant-monitor of Cushgar, had blown more than one entire attacking fleet out of space during its eighty years of operation. Its outer defenses weren't to be breached by any known weapon; and its weapons could hash up a planetary system with no particular effort. The *Glant* was invincible.

It was just a trifle slow, though. And these ghost ships, these ridiculous invaders, were moving at an almost incredible pace! He wouldn't be able to get the *Glant* positioned in time to stop the van.

The Metag scowled. If only the reports had been more specific—and less mysteriously terminated! Three times, in the past five days, border fleets had announced they had detected the van of the ghosts and were prepared to inter-

ept. Each time that had been the last announcement
ceived from the fleet in question! Of course, communica-
ons *could* become temporarily disrupted, in just that in-
tantaneous, wholesale fashion, by perfectly natural distur-
ances—but three times!

A slightly chilled breeze tickled the Metag's back-spines
or a moment. There was no nonsense about the Metag;
ut just the same, his conscience—like that of Cushgar gen-
rally—was riddled enough to be conducive to occasional
uperstitious chills.

"There they are, sir!" the adjutant announced suddenly,
n an excited quaver.

The Metag stared unbelievingly.

It was as bad as the worst of the reports. It was worse!
ecure behind the *Glant's* defenses, the sight of a few thou-
and hostile cruisers wouldn't have caused him a qualm—

But this!

There *were* a few small war vessels among them—none
ver six hundred feet long. But, so far as one could tell
rom their seared, beam-blasted exteriors, most of them
ad been freighters of every possible size, type and descrip-
ion. There was a sprinkling of dainty, badly slashed yachts
nd other personal space craft. No wonder they'd been mis-
aken for the murdered cold hulks of the centuries, swept
long in a current of awful new life—!

But the worst of it was that, mixed up with that stream,
vas stuff which simply didn't belong in space—it should
ave been gliding sedately over the surface of some plane-
ary sea! Some, by Old Webolt, had *wings!*

And that one, there!

"It's a *house!*" the Metag howled, in horrified recogni-
on. "A thundering, Old-Webolt-damned HOUSE!"

House and all, the battered ghost-horde came flashing up
t a pace that couldn't have been matched by Cushgar's
ewest destroyers. Ponderously and enormously, the *Glant*
aced forward in what was, even now, an obviously futile
ttempt to meet them.

The adjutant was gabbling at his side.

"Sir, we may just be able to reach their flank with the grapnels before they're past!"

"Get them out!" the Metag roared. "Full range! Get them out! We've got to stop one of them—find out! It's a masquerade—"

They didn't quite make it. Near the end of the van, a torpedo-shaped, blackened *thing* seemed to be touched for a moment by a grapnel beam's tip. It was whirled about in a monstrous semicircle, then darted off at a tangent and shot away after the others. They vanished in the direction of Cushgar's heart-cluster.

"*That* was a mistake!" breathed the Metag. "It'll be telling them about us. If the main body deflects its course, we'll never . . . no, wait! There's one more coming—stop it NOW!"

A slender, three-hundred-foot space yacht flashed headlong into a cluster of the *Glant's* grapnels and freezers and stopped dead.

"And *now!*" The Metag passed a broad tongue over his trembling lips. "*Now* we'll find out! Bring them in!"

Grapnels and tractors began to maneuver the little yacht in carefully through the intricate maze of passages between the *Glant's* overlapping first, second, and third defense zones. There was nothing wrong with this ghost's looks; it gleamed blue and silver and unblemished in the lights glaring upon it from a hundred different directions. It might have taken off ten minutes before on its maiden flight.

The Great Squid of space had caught itself a shining minnow.

"Sir," the adjutant said uneasily, "mightn't it be better to beam it first?"

The Metag stared at him.

"And kill whoever's inside before we've talked to them?" he inquired carefully. "Have you gone mad? Does that look like a battleship to you—or do you think they *are* ghosts? It's the wildest good luck we caught them. If it hadn't come straight at us, as if it wanted to be caught—"

He paused a moment, scowling out through the screens at the yacht which now hung in a bundle of guide beams

ust above the *Glant's* yawning intake-port. The minnow
was about to be swallowed.

"As if it *wanted* to be caught?" he repeated doubtfully.

It was the last doubt he had.

The little yacht moved.

It moved out of the grapnels and tractors and freezers
as if there weren't any! It slid over the monitor's spindle
length inside its defenses like a horrible caress. Behind it,
the *Glant's* multiple walls folded back in a white-hot, thick-
lipped wound. The *Glant* split down its length like a giant
clam, opened out and spilled its flaming, exploding guts into
space.

The little yacht darted on, unblemished, to resume its
outrider position on the ghost-van's flank.

Zone Agent Pagadan of Lar-Sancaya really earned herself a chunk of immortal glory that day! But, unfortunately,
no trace of the *Glant* was ever discovered again. And so
no one would believe her, though she swore to the truth
on a stack of Lar-Sancaya's holiest writings and on seven
different lie detectors. Everyone knew what Pagadan could
do to a lie detector, and as for the other—

Well, there remained a reasonable doubt.

"What about your contact with the ghosts—the invaders?"
Cushgar called to the invincible *Glant*. "Have you stopped
them? Destroyed them?"

The *Glant* gave no answer.

Cushgar called the *Glant*. Cushgar called the *Glant*. Cushgar called the *Glant*. Cushgar called the *Glant*—

Cushgar stared, appalled, into its night-sky and listened.
Some millions of hostile stars stared back with icy disdain.
Not a cry came again from the *Glant*—not a whisper!

The main body of the ghost fleet passed the spot twenty
minutes later. It looked hardly damaged at all. In its approximate center was Zone Agent Zamman Tarradang-Pok's
black globe, and inside the globe Zamm lay in Deep Rest.
Her robot knew its duty—it would arouse her the instant
it made hostile contact. It had passed through a third of
Cushgar's territory by now, but it hadn't made any as yet.

The main body overtook the eager beavers up front eight

hours later and merged with them. Straggled groups came
up at intervals from behind and joined. The ghost fleet
formed into a single cluster—

A hell-wind blew from the Galaxy's center on Cushgar's
heart; and panic rushed before it. The dead were coming:
the slaughtered billions, the shattered hulks, the broken de-
fenders—joined now in a monstrous, unstoppable army of
judgment that outsped sane thought!

Cushgar panicked—and the good, solid strategy of centuries was lost. Nightmare was plunging at it! Scattered fleet
after fleet, ship after ship, it hurled what it could grab up
into the path of the ghosts.

Not a cry, not a whisper, came back from the sacrifices!

Then the remaining fleets refused to move.

Zamm was having a nice dream.

It didn't surprise her particularly. Deep Rest was mostly
dreamless; but at some levels it produced remarkably vivid
and detailed effects. On more than one occasion they'd even
tricked her into thinking they were real!

This time her ship appeared to have docked itself somewhere. The somno-cabin was still darkened, but the rest of
it was all lit up. There were a lot of voices.

Zamm zipped up the side of her coverall suit and sat
up on the edge of the couch. She listened a moment, and
laughed. This one was going to be silly but nice!

"Box cars again!" a woman's voice shouted in the control room as Zamm came down the passage from her cabin.
"You crummy, white-whiskered, cheating old—" A round
of applause drowned out the last word, or words.

"Lady or no lady," the voice of Senator Thartwith rose
in sonorous indignation, "one more such crack and I mow
you down!"

The applause went up a few decibels.

"And here's Zamm!" someone yelled.

They were all around her suddenly. Zamm grinned at
them, embarrassed. "Glad you found the drinks!" she murmured.

The tall Goddess of Amuth, still flushed from her argu-

nt with Zone Agent Thartwith, scooped Zamm up from
ind and set her on the edge of a table.

"Where's a glass for Zamm?"

She sipped it slowly, looking them over. There they
re, the tricky and tough ones—the assassins and hunters
 organizers and spies! The Co-ordinator's space pack,
innermost circle. There he was himself!

"Hi, Bent!" she said, respecting his mission-alias even in
dream. "Hi, Weems! . . . Hi, Ferd!" she nodded around
 circle between sips.

Two score of them or more, come into Deep Rest to
 her good-by! She'd bought them all their lives, at one
 e or another; and they'd bought her hers. But she'd never
 n more than three together at any one time in reality.
ok a dream to gather them all!

Zamm laughed.

"Nice party!" she smiled. Nice dream. She put down her
pty glass.

"That's it!" said the Goddess Loppos. She swung Zamm's
 t up on the table, and pulled her around by the shoulders
 look at the wall. There was a vision port there, but it
 s closed.

"What's all this?" Zamm smiled expectantly, lying back
Loppos' arms. What goofy turn would it take now?

The vision port clicked open. Harsh daylight streamed in.
The ship seemed to have set itself down in a sort of hot,
dy park. There was a huge gray building in the back-
und. Zamm gazed at the building, the smile going slowly
m her lips. A hospital, wasn't it? Where'd she seen—?

Her eyes darted suddenly to the lower left corner of the
rt. The edge of another building was visible there—a
all house it was, also gray and very close. It would be
ht beside the ship!

Zamm convulsed.

"No!" she screamed. "It's a dream!"

She was being lifted from the table and put on her
 t. Her knees wobbled, then stiffened.

"They're feeling fine, Zamm," the voice of the gray-
ired man called Bent was saying. He added: "The boy's
 t pretty big."

"She'll be all right now," somebody else murmured behind her. "Zamm, you know Deep Rest! We couldn't take chances with it. We told them they'd have to wait there in the house till you woke."

The ramp beam set her down on the sand of a path. There was hot daylight around her then—seventeen years behind her, and an open door twenty steps ahead.

Her knees began wobbling again.

Zamm couldn't move.

For a score of scores of light-years about, Cushgar the Mighty lay on its face, howling to its gods to save it from the wrath of the ghosts and the wrath of Zamm.

But she—Zone Agent Zamman Tarradang-Pok, conqueror of space, time, and all the laws of probability—she, Free mind Unqualified of the Free Daya-Bals—Doctor of Neuronics—Vega's grand champion of the Galaxy:

No, she just couldn't move!

Something *put-putted* suddenly by overhead. Enough of its seared and molten exterior remained to indicate that at some earlier stage of its career it might have been a fairly amiable-looking freighter. But there was nothing amiable about its appearance now! It looked like a wreck that had rolled for a century in the fires of hell, and put in another decade or two sunk deep in an acid sea. It looked, in fact, exactly as a ship might expect to look whose pilot had a weakness for withholding his fire till he was well within point-blank range.

But though it had lost its make-up, the ship was otherwise still in extra-good condition! It passed over Zamm's head, bobbed up and down twice in cheerful greeting, and went *putting* off on its secondaries, across the vast hospital and toward the city beyond, dropping a bit as it went, to encourage Cushgar to howl a little louder.

Zamm gazed blankly after the beat-up, impossible warrior, and heard herself laughing. She took a step—and another step.

Why, sure, she could move!

She was running—

". . . so that's how it was," the Third Co-ordinator told Bropha. He swirled the contents of his nearly empty glass around gently, raised it and finished his drink. "All we'd really intended was to hold that dead-straight course, and smash their light interception all the way in. That was to make sure they'd bunch every heavy ship they had on that line, to stop us just before we reached the Cluster.

"Then we were going to pop off at an angle, streak for the place they were keeping Zamm's folks, grab them up and get out of Cushgar again—

"But, of course," he added, "when we discovered they'd all rolled over on their back spikes and were waving their hands in the air, we couldn't resist taking over! You just never know what you start when you go off on an impromptu mission like that!"

He paused and frowned, and sighed. For the Third Co-ordinator was a man of method, who liked to see a job well worked out in advance, with all its angles considered and plenty of allowance made for any unforeseeable developments.

"How about a second drink?" Bropha inquired.

"No," said his friend; "I've got to get back to work. They can squawk all they like"—Bropha realized he was referring to his colleagues of the Council—"but there isn't another Department of the Confederacy that's been jammed up by the Cushgar affair as badly as Galactic Zones is right now! That was forty-two thousand two hundred and thirty-eight individual mission-schedules we had to re-plot!" he said, still somewhat aghast at the completeness of the jam. "Only a third of it's done! And afterwards, I'll have time to worry about finding a replacement for Zamm. There's nothing so scarce as a really good Peripheral Agent! That's all *I* got out of it—"

Bropha looked sympathetic.

"I talked to that boy, and I've got some hopes for him," the Co-ordinator added glumly. "If she keeps her promise, that is, and lets him come to Jeltad, by and by. But he'll never be like Zamm!"

"Give him time," Bropha said consolingly. "They grow up slowly. They're a long-lived race, the Daya-Bals."

"I thought of that, too!" the Co-ordinator nodded. "She'll

raise a dozen now before she's done; and among them there might be one, or two— But, by the way she talked, I knew right then Zamm would never let any of the others go beyond fifty light-years of Betelgeuse!"

THE SECOND NIGHT
OF SUMMER

ON THE night after the day that brought summer officially to the land of Wend, on the planet of Noorhut, the shining lights were seen again in the big hollow at the east end of Grimp's father's farm.

Grimp watched them for more than an hour from his upstairs room. The house was dark, but an occasional murmur of voices floated up to him through the windows below. Everyone in the farmhouse was looking at the lights.

On the other farms around and in the village, which was over a hill and another two miles up the valley, every living soul who could get within view of the hollow was probably doing the same. For a time, the agitated yelling of the Village Guardian's big pank-hound had sounded clearly over the hill, but he had quieted down then very suddenly— or had *been* quieted down, more likely, Grimp suspected. The Guardian was dead-set against anyone making a fuss about the lights—and that included the pank-hound, too.

There was some excuse for the pank-hound's excitement, though. From the window, Grimp could see there were a lot more lights tonight than had turned up in previous years—big, brilliant-blue bubbles, drifting and rising and falling silently all about the hollow. Sometimes one would lift straight up for several hundred feet, or move

157

off over the edge of the hollow for about the same distance, and hang there suspended for a few minutes, before floating back to the others. That was as far as they ever went away from the hollow.

There was, in fact, no need for the Halpa detector-globes to go any farther than that to get the information wanted by those who had sent them out, and who were listening now to the steady flow of brief reports, in some Halpa equivalent of human speech-thought, coming back to them through the globes:

"No signs of hostile activity in the vicinity of the breakthrough point. No weapons or engines of power within range of detection. The area shows no significant alterations since the last investigation. Sharp curiosity among those who observe us consciously—traces of alarm and suspicion. But no overt hostility."

The reports streamed on without interruption, repeating the same bits of information automatically and incessantly, while the globes floated and dipped soundlessly above and about the hollow.

Grimp continued to watch them, blinking sleepily now and then, until a spreading glow over the edge of the valley announced that Noorhut's Big Moon was coming up slowly, like a Planetary Guardian, to make its own inspection of the lights. The globes began to dim out then, just as they always had done at moonrise in the preceding summers; and even before the top rim of the Big Moon's yellow disk edged over the hills, the hollow was completely dark.

Grimp heard his mother starting up the stairs. He got hurriedly into bed. The show was over for the night and he had a lot a pleasant things to think about before he went to sleep.

Now that the lights had showed up, his good friend Grandma Erisa Wannattel and her patent-medicine trailer were sure to arrive, too. Sometime late tomorrow afternoon, the big draft-trailer would come rolling up the valley road from the city. For that was what Grandma Wannattel had done the past four summers—ever since the lights first started appearing above the hollow for the few nights they were to be seen there each year. And since four years were exactly half of Grimp's whole life, that made Grandma's return a mathematical certainty for him.

Other people, of course, like the Village Guardian, might have a poor opinion of Grandma, but just hanging around her and the trailer and the gigantic, exotic-looking rhinocerine pony that pulled it was, in Grimp's opinion, a lot better even than going to the circus.

And vacations started the day after tomorrow! The whole future just now, in fact, looked like one good thing after another, extending through a vista of summery infinities.

Grimp went to sleep happily.

At about the same hour, though at a distance greater than Grimp's imagination had stretched as yet, eight large ships came individually out of the darkness between the stars that was their sea, and began to move about Noorhut in a carefully timed pattern of orbits. They stayed much too far out to permit any instrument of space-detection to suspect that Noorhut might be their common center of interest.

But that was what it was. Though the men who crewed the eight ships bore the people of Noorhut no ill will, hardly anything could have looked less promising for Noorhut than the cargo they had on board.

Seven of them were armed with a gas which was not often used any more. A highly volatile lethal catalyst, it sank to the solid surface of a world over which it was freed and spread out swiftly there to the point where its presence could no longer be detected by any chemical means. However, its effect of drawing the final breath almost imperceptibly out of all things that were oxygen-breathing was not noticeably reduced by diffusion.

The eighth ship was equipped with a brace of torpedoes, which were normally released some hours after the gas-carriers dispersed their invisible death. They were quite small torpedoes, since the only task remaining for them would be to ignite the surface of the planet that had been treated with the catalyst.

All those things might presently happen to Noorhut. But they would happen only if a specific message was flashed from it to the circling squadron—the message that Noorhut already was lost to a deadly foe who must, at any cost now, be prevented from spreading out from it to other inhabited worlds.

Next afternoon, right after school, as Grimp came expectantly around the bend of the road at the edge of the farm, he found the village policeman sitting there on a rock, gazing tearfully down the road.

"Hello, Runny," said Grimp, disturbed. Considered in the light of gossip he'd overheard in the village that morning, this didn't look so good for Grandma. It just didn't look good.

The policeman blew his nose on a handkerchief he carried tucked into the front of his uniform, wiped his eyes, and gave Grimp an annoyed glance.

"Don't *you* call me Runny, Grimp!" he said, replacing the handkerchief. Like Grimp himself and most of the people on Noorhut, the policeman was brown-skinned and dark-eyed, normally a rather good-looking young fellow. But his eyes were swollen and red-rimmed now; and his nose, which as a bit larger than average, anyway, was also red and swollen and undeniably runny. He had hay-fever bad.

Grimp apologized and sat down thoughtfully on the rock beside the policeman, who was one of his numerous cousins. He was about to mention that he had overheard Vellit using the expression when she and the policeman came through the big Leeth-flower orchard above the farm the other evening—at a much less leisurely rate than was their custom there. But he thought better of it. Vellit was the policeman's girl for most of the year, but she broke their engagement regularly during hay-fever season and called him cousin instead of dearest.

"What are you doing here?" Grimp asked bluntly instead.

"Waiting," said the policeman.

"For what?" said Grimp, with a sinking heart.

"Same individual you are, I guess," the policeman told him, hauling out the handkerchief again. He blew. "This year she's going to go right back where she came from or get pinched."

"Who says so?" scowled Grimp.

"The Guardian, that's who," said the policeman. "That good enough for you?"

"He can't do it!" Grimp said hotly. "It's our farm and she's got all her licenses."

"He's had a whole year to think up a new list she's got to have." the policeman informed him. He fished in the breast-pocket of his uniform; pulled out a folded paper and opened it. "He put thirty-four items down here I got to check—she's bound to miss on one of them."

"It's a dirty trick!" said Grimp, rapidly scanning as much as he could see of the list.

"Let's us have more respect for the Village Guardian, Grimp!" the policeman said warningly.

"Uh-huh," muttered Grimp. "Sure . . . " If Runny would just move his big thumb out of the way. But what a list! Trailer; rhinocerine pony (beast, heavy draft, imported); patent medicines; household utensils; fortune-telling; pets; herbs; miracle-healing—

The policeman looked down, saw what Grimp was doing and raised the paper out of his line of vision. "That's an official document," he said, warding Grimp off with one hand and tucking the paper away with the other. "Let's us not get our dirty hands on it."

Grimp was thinking fast. Grandma Wannattel did have framed licenses for some of the items he'd read hanging around inside the trailer, but certainly not thirty-four of them.

"Remember that big skinless werret I caught last season?" he asked.

The policeman gave him a quick glance, looked away again and wiped his eyes thoughtfully. The season on werrets would open the following week and he was as ardent a fisherman as anyone in the village—and last summer Grimp's monster werret had broken a twelve-year record in the valley.

"Some people," Grimp said idly, staring down the valley road to the point where it turned into the woods, "would sneak after a person for days who's caught a big werret, hoping he'd be dumb enough to go back to that pool."

The policeman flushed and dabbed the handkerchief gingerly at his nose.

"Some people would even sit in a haystack and use spyglasses, even when the hay made them sneeze like crazy," continued Grimp quietly.

The policeman's flush deepened. He sneezed.

"But a person isn't that dumb," said Grimp. "Not when he knows there's anyway two werrets there six inches bigger than the one he caught."

"*Six inches?*" the policeman repeated a bit incredulously— eagerly.

"Easy," nodded Grimp. "I had a look at them again last week."

It was the policeman's turn to think. Grimp idly hauled out his slingshot, fished a pebble out of his small-pebble pocket and knocked the head off a flower twenty feet away. He yawned negligently.

"You're pretty good with that slingshot," the policeman remarked. "You must be just about as good as the culprit that used a slingshot to ring the fire-alarm signal on the defense unit bell from the top of the school house last week."

"That'd take a pretty good shot," Grimp admitted.

"And who then," continued the policeman, "dropped pepper in his trail, so the pank-hound near coughed off his head when we started to track him. The Guardian," he added significantly, "would like to have a clue about that culprit, all right."

"Sure, sure," said Grimp, bored. The policeman, the Guardian, and probably even the pank-hound, knew exactly who the culprit was; but they wouldn't be able to prove it in twenty thousand years. Runny just had to realize first that threats weren't going to get him anywhere near a record werret.

Apparently, he had; he was settling back for another bout of thinking. Grimp, interested in what he would produce next, decided just to leave him to it. . . .

Then Grimp jumped up suddenly from the rock.

"There they are!" he yelled, waving the slingshot.

A half-mile down the road, Grandma Wannattel's big, silvery trailer had come swaying out of the woods behind the hinocerine pony and turned up toward the farm. The pony aw Grimp, lifted its head, which was as long as a tall man, nd bawled a thunderous greeting. Grandma Wannattel stood p on the driver's seat and waved a green silk handkerchief.

Grimp started sprinting down the road.

The werrets should turn the trick—but he'd better get Grandma informed, just the same, about recent developments ere, before she ran into Runny.

Grandma Wannattel flicked the pony's horny rear with the eins just before they reached the policeman, who was wait-ag at the side of the road with the Guardian's check-list un-olded in his hand.

The pony broke into a lumbering trot, and the trailer swept ast Runny and up around the bend of the road, where it topped well within the boundaries of the farm. They climbed own and Grandma quickly unhitched the pony. It waddled, runting, off the road and down into the long, marshy mead-w above the hollow. It stood still there, cooling its feet.

Grimp felt a little better. Getting the trailer off community roperty gave Grandma a technical advantage. Grimp's people ad a favorable opinion of her, and they were a sturdy lot ho enjoyed telling off the Guardian any time he didn't ac-ually have a law to back up his orders. But on the way to e farm, she had confessed to Grimp that, just as he'd feared, e didn't have anything like thirty-four licenses. And now e policeman was coming up around the bend of the road fter them, blowing his nose and frowning.

"Just let me handle him alone," Grandma told Grimp out f the corner of her mouth.

He nodded and strolled off into the meadow to pass the me with the pony. She'd had a lot of experience in handling olicemen.

"Well, well, young man," he heard her greeting his cousin ehind him. "That looks like a bad cold you've got."

The policeman sneezed.

"Wish it were a cold," he said resignedly. "It's hay-fever. an't do a thing with it. Now I've got a list here—"

"Hay-fever?" said Grandma. "Step up into the trailer a oment. We'll fix that."

"About this list—" began Runny, and stopped. "You think you got something that would fix it?" he asked skeptically. "I've been to I don't know how many doctors and they didn't help any."

"Doctors!" said Grandma. Grimp heard her heels click up the metal steps that led into the back of the trailer. "Come right in, won't take a moment."

"Well—" said Runny doubtfully, but he followed her inside.

Grimp winked at the pony. The first round went to Grandma.

"Hello, pony," he said.

His worries couldn't reduce his appreciation of Grandma's fabulous draft-animal. Partly, of course, it was just that it was such an enormous beast. The long, round barrel of its body rested on short legs with wide, flat feet which were settled deep in the meadow's mud by now. At one end was a spiky tail, and at the other a very big, wedge-shaped head, with a blunt, badly chipped horn set between nose and eyes. From nose to tail and all around, it was covered with thick, rectangular, horny plates, a mottled green-brown in color.

Grimp patted its rocky side affectionately. He loved the pony most for being the ugliest thing that had ever showed up on Noorhut. According to Grandma, she had bought it from a bankrupt circus which had imported it from a planet called Treebel; and Treebel was supposed to be a world full of hot swamps, inexhaustibly explosive volcanoes and sulphurous stenches.

One might have thought that after wandering around melting lava and under rainfalls of glowing ashes for most of its life, the pony would have considered Noorhut pretty tame. But though there wasn't much room for expression around the solid slab of bone supporting the horn, which was the front of its face, Grimp thought it looked thoroughly contented with its feet sunk out of sight in Noorhut's cool mud.

"You're a big fat pig!" he told it fondly.

The pony slobbered out a long, purple tongue and carefully parted his hair.

"Cut it out!" said Grimp. "Ugh!"

The pony snorted, pleased, curled its tongue about a huge clump of weeds, pulled them up and flipped them into its mouth, roots, mud and all. It began to chew.

Grimp glanced at the sun and turned anxiously to study the trailer. If she didn't get rid of Runny soon, they'd be calling him back to the house for supper before he and Grandma got around to having a good talk. And they weren't letting him out of doors these evenings, while the shining lights were here.

He gave the pony a parting whack, returned quietly to the road and sat down out of sight near the back door of the trailer, where he could hear what was going on.

". . . so about the only thing the Guardian could tack on you now," the policeman was saying, "would be a Public Menace charge. If there's any trouble about the lights this year, he's likely to try that. He's not a bad Guardian, you know, but he's got himself talked into thinking you're sort of to blame for the lights showing up here every year."

Grandma chuckled. "Well, I try to get here in time to see them every summer," she admitted. "I can see how that might give him the idea."

"And of course," said the policeman, "we're all trying to keep it quiet about them. If the news got out, we'd be having a lot of people coming here from the city, just to look. No one but the Guardian minds you being here, only you don't want a lot of city people tramping around your farms."

"Of course not," agreed Grandma. "And I certainly haven't told anyone about them myself."

"Last night," the policeman added, "everyone was saying here were twice as many lights this year as last summer. That's what got the Guardian so excited."

Chafing more every minute, Grimp had to listen then to an extended polite argument about how much Runny wanted to pay Grandma for her hay-fever medicines, while she insisted he didn't owe her anything at all. In the end, Grandma lost and the policeman paid up—much too much to take from any friend of Grimp's folks, Grandma protested to the last. And then, finally, that righteous minion of the law came climbing down the trailer steps again, with Grandma following him to the door.

"How do I look, Grimp?" he beamed cheerfully as Grimp stood up.

"Like you ought to wash your face sometime," Grimp said tactlessly, for he was fast losing patience with Runny. But then his eyes widened in surprise.

Under a coating of yellowish grease, Runny's nose seemed to have returned almost to the shape it had out of hay-fever season, and his eyelids were hardly puffed at all! Instead of flaming red, those features, furthermore, now were only a delicate pink in shade. Runny, in short, was almost handsome again.

"Pretty good, eh?" he said. "Just one shot did it. And I've only got to keep the salve on another hour. Isn't that right, Grandma?"

"That's right," smiled Grandma from the door, clinking Runny's money gently out of one hand into the other. "You'll be as good as new then."

"Permanent cure, too," said Runny. He patted Grimp benevolently on the head. "And next week we go werret-fishing, eh, Grimp?" he added greedily.

"I guess so," Grimp said, with a trace of coldness. It was his opinion that Runny could have been satisfied with the hay-fever cure and forgotten about the werrets.

"It's a date!" nodded Runny happily and took his greasy face whistling down the road. Grimp scowled after him, half-minded to reach for the sling shot then and there and let go with a medium stone at the lower rear of the uniform. But probably he'd better not.

"Well, that's that," Grandma said softly.

At that moment, up at the farmhouse, a cow horn went "Whoop-whoop!" across the valley.

"Darn," said Grimp. "I knew it was getting late, with him doing all that talking! Now they're calling me to supper." There were tears of disappointment in his eyes.

"Don't let it fuss you, Grimp," Grandma said consolingly. "Just jump up in here a moment and close your eyes."

Grimp jumped up into the trailer and closed his eyes expectantly.

"Put out your hands." Grandma's voice told him.

He put out his hands, and she pushed them together to form a cup. Then something small and light and furry dropped into them, caught hold of one of Grimp's thumbs, with tiny, cool fingers, and chittered.

Grimp's eyes popped open.

"It's a lortel!" he whispered, overwhelmed.

"It's for you!" Grandma beamed.

Grimp couldn't speak. The lortel looked at him from a tiny, black, human face with large blue eyes set in it, wrapped a long, furry tail twice around his wrist, clung to his thumb with its fingers, and grinned and squeaked.

"It's wonderful!" gasped Grimp. "Can you really teach 'em to talk?"

"Hello," said the lortel.

"That's all it can say so far," Grandma said. "But if you're patient with it, it'll learn more."

"I'll be patient," Grimp promised, dazed. "I saw one at the circus this winter, down the valley at Laggand. They said it could talk, but it never said anything while I was there."

"Hello!" said the lortel.

"Hello!" gulped Grimp.

The cow horn whoop-whooped again.

"I guess you'd better run along to supper, or they might get mad," said Grandma.

"I know," said Grimp. "What does it eat?"

"Bugs and flowers and honey and fruit and eggs, when it's wild. But you just feed it whatever you eat yourself."

"Well, good-by," said Grimp. "And golly—thanks, Grandma."

He jumped out of the trailer. The lortel climbed out of his hand, ran up his arm and sat on his shoulder, wrapping its tail around his neck.

"It knows you already," Grandma said. "It won't run away."

Grimp reached up carefully with his other hand and patted the lortel.

"I'll be back early tomorrow," he said. "No school. . . ."

They won't let me out after supper as long as those lights keep coming around."

The cow horn whooped for the third time, very loudly. This time it meant business.

"Well, good-by," Grimp repeated hastily. He ran off, the lortel hanging on to his shirt collar and squeaking.

Grandma looked after him and then at the sun, which had just touched the tops of the hills with its lower rim.

"Might as well have some supper myself," she remarked, apparently to no one in particular. "But after that I'll have to run out the go-buggy and create a diversion."

Lying on its armor-plated belly down in the meadow, the pony swung its big head around toward her. It's small yellow eyes blinked questioningly.

"What makes you think a diversion will be required?" Its voice asked into her ear. The ability to produce such ventriloquial effects was one of the talents that made the pony well worth its considerable keep to Grandma.

"Weren't you listening?" she scolded. "That policeman told me the Guardian's planning to march the village's defense unit up to the hollow after supper, and start them shooting at the Halpa detector-globes as soon as they show up."

The pony swore an oath meaningless to anyone who hadn't been raised on the planet Treebel. It stood up, braced itself, and began pulling its feet out of the mud in a succession of loud, sucking noises.

"I haven't had an hour's straight rest since you talked me into tramping around with you eight years ago!" it complained.

"But you've certainly been seeing life, like I promised," Grandma smiled.

The pony slopped in a last, enormous tongueful of wet weeds. "That I have!" it said, with emphasis.

It came chewing up to the road.

"I'll keep a watch on things while you're having your supper," it told her.

As the uniformed twelve-man defense unit marched in good order out of the village, on its way to assume a strategic position around the hollow on Grimp's father's farm, there was a sudden, small explosion not very far off.

The Guardian, who was marching in the lead with a gun over his shoulder and the slavering pank-hound on a leash, stopped short. The unit broke ranks and crowded up behind him.

"What was that?" the Guardian inquired.

Everybody glanced questioningly around the rolling green slopes of the valley, already darkened with evening shadows. The pank-hound sat down before the Guardian, pointed its nose at the even darker shadows in the woods ahead of them and growled.

"Look!" a man said, pointing in the same direction.

A spark of bright green light had appeared on their path, just where it entered the woods. The spark grew rapidly in size, became as big as a human head—then bigger! Smoky green streamers seemed to be pouring out of it. . . .

"I'm going home right now," someone announced at that point, sensibly enough.

"Stand your ground!" the Guardian ordered, conscious of the beginnings of a general withdrawal movement behind him. He was an old soldier. He unslung his gun, cocked it and pointed it. The pank-hound got up on his six feet and bristled.

"Stop!" the Guardian shouted at the green light.

It expanded promptly to the size of a barrrel, new steamers shooting out from it and fanning about like hungry tentacles.

He fired.

"Run!" everybody yelled then. The pank-hound slammed backward against the Guardian's legs, upsetting him, and streaked off after the retreating unit. The green light had spread outward jerkily into the shape of something like a many-armed, writhing starfish, almost the size of the trees about it. Deep, hooting sounds came out of it as it started drifting down the path toward the Guardian.

He got up on one knee and, in a single drumroll of sound, emptied all thirteen charges remaining in his gun into the middle of the starfish. It hooted more loudly, waved its arms more wildly, and continued to advance.

He stood up quickly then, slung the gun over his shoulder and joined the retreat. By the time the unit reached the first houses of the village, he was well up in the front ranks again. And a few minutes later, he was breathlessly organizing the local defenses, employing the tactics that had shown their worth in the raids of the Laggand Bandits nine years before.

The starfish, however, was making no attempt to follow up the valley people's rout. It was still on the path at the point where the Guardian had seen it last, waving its arms about and hooting menacingly at the silent trees.

"That should do it, I guess," Grandma Wannattel said. "Before the first projection fizzles out, the next one in the chain will start up where they can see it from the village. It ought to be past midnight before anyone starts bothering about the globes again. Particularly since there aren't going to be any globes around tonight—that is, if the Halpa attack-schedule has been correctly estimated."

"I wish we were safely past midnight right now," the rhinocerine pony worriedly informed her. Its dark shape stood a little up the road from the trailer, outlined motionlessly like a ponderous statue against the red evening sky. Its head was up; it looked as if it were listening. Which it was, in its own way—listening for any signs of activity from the hollow.

"No sense getting anxious about it," Grandma remarked. She was perched on a rock at the side of the road, a short distance from the pony, with a small black bag slung over her shoulder. "We'll wait here another hour till it's good and dark and then go down to the hollow. The breakthrough might begin a couple of hours after that."

"It *would* have to be us again!" grumbled the pony. In spite of its size, its temperament was on the nervous side. And while any companion of Zone Agent Wannattel was bound to run regularly into situations that were far from soothing, the pony couldn't recall any previous experience that had looked as extremely unsoothing as the prospects of the night-hours ahead. On far-off Vega's world of Jeltad, in the planning offices of the Department of Galactic Zones, the decision to put Noorhut at stake to win one round in mankind's grim war with the alien and mysterious Halpa might have seemed as distressing as it was unavoidable. But the pony couldn't help feeling that the distress would have become a little more acute if Grandma's distant employers had happened to be standing right here with the two of them while the critical hours approached.

"I'd feel a lot better myself if Headquarters hadn't picked us for this particular operation," Grandma admitted. "Us and Noorhut. . . ."

Because, by what was a rather singular coincidence, considering how things stood there tonight, the valley was also Grandma's home. She had been born, quite some while before, a hundred and eighty miles farther inland, at the foot of the dam of the great river Wend, which had given its name to the land, and nowadays supplied it with almost all its required power.

Erisa Wannattel had done a great deal of traveling since she first became aware of the fact that her varied abilities and adventuresome nature needed a different sort of task to absorb them than could be found on Noorhut, which was progressing placidly up into the final stages of a rounded and balanced planetary civilization. But she still liked to consider the Valley of the Wend as her home and headquarters, to which she returned as often as her work would permit. Her exact understanding of the way people there thought about things and did things also made them easy for her to manipulate; and on occasion that could be very useful.

In most other places, the means she had employed to turn the Guardian and his troop back from the hollow probably would have started a panic or brought armed ships and radiation guns zooming up for the kill within minutes. But the valley people had considered it just another local emergency. The bronze alarm bell in the village had pronounced a state of siege, and cow horns passed the word up to the outlying farms. Within minutes, the farmers were pelting down the roads to the village with their families and guns; and, very soon afterward, everything quieted down again. Guard lines had been set up by then, with

the women and children quartered in the central buildings,
while the armed men had settled down to watching Grandma's illusion projections—directional video narrow beams—
from the discreet distance marked by the village boundaries.

If nothing else happened, the people would just stay there
till morning and then start a cautious investigation. After
seeing mysterious blue lights dancing harmlessly over Grimp's
farm for four summers, this section of Wend was pretty
well conditioned to fiery apparitions. But even if they got
too adventurous, they couldn't hurt themselves on the projections, which were designed to be nothing but very effective visual displays.

What it all came to was that Grandma had everybody
in the neighborhood rounded up and immobilized where
she wanted them.

In every other respect, the valley presented an exceptionally peaceful twilight scene to the eye. There was nothing to show that it was the only present point of contact
between forces engaged in what was probably a war of
intergalactic proportions—a war made wraithlike but doubly
deadly by the circumstance that, in over a thousand years,
neither side had found out much more about the other than
the merciless and devastating finality of its forms of attack.
There never had been any actual battles between Mankind
and the Halpa, only alternate and very thorough massacres
—all of them, from Mankind's point of view, on the wrong
side of the fence.

The Halpa alone had the knowledge that enabled them
to reach their human adversary. That was the trouble. But,
apparently, they could launch their attacks only by a supreme effort, under conditions that existed for periods of
less than a score of years, and about three hundred years
apart as Mankind measured time.

It was hard to find any good in them, other than the
virtue of persistence. Every three hundred years, they punctually utilized that brief period to execute one more thrust,
carefully prepared and placed, and carried out with a dreadfully complete abruptness, against some new point of human

civilization—and this time the attack was going to come through on Noorhut.

"Something's starting to move around in that hollow!" the pony announced suddenly. "It's not one of their globe-detectors."

"I know," murmured Grandma. "That's the first of the Halpa themselves. They're going to be right on schedule, it seems. But don't get nervous. They can't hurt anything until their transmitter comes through and revives them. We've got to be particularly careful now not to frighten them off. They seem to be even more sensitive to emotional tensions in their immediate surroundings than the globes."

The pony made no reply. It knew what was at stake and why eight big ships were circling Noorhut somewhere beyond space-detection tonight. It knew, too, that the ships would act only if it was discovered that Grandma had failed. But—

The pony shook its head uneasily. The people on Treebel had never become civilized to the point of considering the possibility of taking calculated risks on a planetary scale—not to mention the fact that the lives of the pony and of Grandma were included in the present calculation. In the eight years it had been accompanying her on her travels, it had developed a tremendous respect for Erisa Wannattel's judgment and prowess. But, just the same, frightening the Halpa off, if it still could be done, seemed like a very sound idea right now to the pony.

As a matter of fact, as Grandma well knew, it probably could have been done at this stage by tossing a small firecracker into the hollow. Until they had established their planetary foothold, the Halpa took extreme precautions. They could spot things in the class of radiation weapons a hundred miles away, and either that or any suggestion of local aggressiveness or of long-range observation would check the invasion attempt on Noorhut then and there.

But one of the principal reasons she was here tonight was to see that nothing *did* happen to stop it. For this assault would only be diverted against some other world then, and quite probably against one where the significance of the spying detector-globes wouldn't be understood before it was too late. The best information system in the Galaxy couldn't keep more than an insignificant fraction of its population on the alert for dangers like that—

She bounced suddenly to her feet and, at the same instant, the pony swung away from the hollow toward which it had been staring. They both stood for a moment then, turning their heads about, like baffled hounds trying to fix a scent on the wind.

"It's Grimp!" Grandma exclaimed.

The rhinocerine pony snorted faintly. "Those are his thought images, all right," it agreed. "He seems to feel you need protection. Can you locate him?"

"Not yet," said Grandma anxiously. "Yes, I can. He's coming up through the woods on the other side of the hollow, off to the left. The little devil!" She was hustling back to the trailer. "Come on, I'll have to ride you there. I can't even dare use the go-buggy this late in the day."

The pony crouched beside the trailer while she quickly snapped on its saddle from the top of the back steps. Six metal rings had been welded into the horny plates of its back for this purpose, so it was a simple job. Grandma clambered aloft, hanging onto the saddle's hand-rails.

"Swing wide of the hollow!" she warned. "This could spoil everything. But make all the noise you want. The Halpa don't care about noise as such—it has to have emotional content before they get interested—and the quicker Grimp spots us, the easier it will be to find him."

The pony already was rushing down into the meadow at an amazing rate of speed—it took a lot of very efficient muscle to drive as heavy a body as that through the gluey swamps of Treebel. It swung wide of the hollow and of what it contained, crossed a shallow bog farther down the meadow with a sound like a charging torpedo-boat, and reached the woods.

It had to slow down then, to avoid brushing off Grandma.

"Grimp's down that slope somewhere," Grandma said. "He's heard us."

"They're making a lot of noise!" Grimp's thought reached

m suddenly and clearly. He seemed to be talking to meone. "But we're not scared of them, are we?"

"Bang-bang!" another thought-voice came excitedly.

"It's the lortel," Grandma and the pony said together.

"That's the stuff!", Grimp resumed approvingly. "We'll ng-shoot them all if they don't watch out. But we'd better d Grandma soon."

"Grimp!" shouted Grandma. The pony backed her up th a roaring call.

"Hello?" came the lortel's thought.

"Wasn't that the pony?" asked Grimp. "All right—let's that way."

"Here we come, Grimp!" Grandma shouted as the pony scended the steep side of a ravine with the straight-rward technique of a rockslide.

"That's Grandma!" thought Grimp. "Grandma!" he yelled. ook out! There's monsters all around!"

"What you missed!" yelled Grimp, dancing around the ny as Grandma Wannattel scrambled down from the ddle. "There's monsters all around the village and the uardian killed one and I slingshot another till he fizzled t and I was coming to find you—"

"Your mother will be worried!" began Grandma as they shed into each other's arms.

"No," grinned Grimp. "All the kids are supposed to be eping in the school house and she won't look there till orning and the schoolteacher said the monsters were all" he slowed down cautiously—"ho-lucy-nations. But he ouldn't go look when the Guardian said they'd show him e. He stayed right in bed. But the Guardian's all right— killed one and I slingshot another and the lortel learned new word. Say 'bang-bang,' lortel!" he invited.

"Hello!" squeaked the lortel.

"Aw," said Grimp disappointedly. "He can say it, though. d I've come to take you to the village so the monsters n't get you. Hello, pony!"

"Bang-bang," said the lortel, distinctly.

"See?" cried Grimp. "He isn't scared at all—he's a real ave lortel! If we see some monsters don't you get scared

either, because I've got my slingshot," he said, waving i
blood-thirstily, "and two back pockets still full of mediur
stones. The way to do it is to kill them all!"

"It sounds like a pretty good idea, Grimp," Grandm
agreed. "But you're awfully tired now."

"No, I'm not!" Grimp said surprised. His right eye sagge
shut and then his left; and he opened them both with a
effort and looked at Grandma.

"That's right," he admitted. "I am . . ."

"In fact," said Grandma, "you're asleep!"

"No, I'm n——" objected Grimp. Then he sagged towar
the ground, and Grandma caught him.

"In a way I hate to do it," she panted, wrestling hir
aboard the pony which had lain down and flattened itself a
much as it could to make it easier. "He'd probably enjo
it. But we can't take a chance. He's a husky little devi
too," she groaned, giving a final boost, "and those ammun
tion pockets don't make him any lighter!" She clambere
up again herself and noticed that the lortel had transferre
itself to her coat collar.

The pony stood up cautiously.

"Now what?" it said.

"Might as well go straight to the hollow," said Grandm
breathing hard. "We'll probably have to wait around ther
a few hours, but if we're careful it won't do any harm."

"Did you find a good deep pond?" Grandma asked th
pony a little later, as it came squishing up softly throug
the meadow behind her to join her at the edge of th
hollow.

"Yes," said the pony. "About a hundred yards bacl
That should be close enough. How much more waiting d
you think we'll have to do?"

Grandma shrugged carefully. She was sitting in the gras
with what, by daylight, would have been a good view o
the hollow below. Grimp was asleep with his head on he
knees; and the lortel, after catching a few bugs in the gras
and eating them, had settled down on her shoulder an
dozed off too.

"I don't know," she said. "It's still three hours till Bi

oonrise, and it's bound to be some time before then.
ow you've found a waterhole, we'll just stay here together
d wait. The one thing to remember is not to let yourself
art getting excited about them."

The pony stood huge and chunky beside her, its fore-
et on the edge of the hollow, staring down. Muddy water
ickled from its knobby flanks. It had brought the warm
ud-smells of a summer pond back with it to hang in a
oud about them.

There was vague, dark, continuous motion at the bot-
m of the hollow. A barely noticeable stirring in the single
g pool of darkness that filled it.

"If I were alone," the pony said, "I'd get out of here! I
iow when I ought to be scared. But you've taken psycho-
gical control of my reactions, haven't you?"

"Yes," said Grandma. "It'll be easier for me, though, if
ou help along as much as you can. There's really no danger
itil their transmitter has come through."

"Unless," said the pony, "they've worked out some brand-
ew tricks in the past few hundred years."

"There's that," Grandma admitted. "But they've never
ied changing their tricks on us yet. If it were *us* doing
ie attacking, we'd vary our methods each time, as much
s we could. But the Halpa don't seem to think just like
e do about anything. They wouldn't still be so careful if
iey didn't realize they were very vulnerable at this point."

"I hope they're right about that!" the pony said briefly.

Its head moved then, following the motion of something
iat sailed flutteringly out of the depths of the hollow, cir-
ed along its far rim, and descended again. The inhabi-
ints of Treebel had a much deeper range of dark-vision
ian Grandma Wannattel, but she was also aware of that
iape.

"They're not much to look at," the pony remarked. "Like
big, dark rag of leather, mostly."

"Their physical structure is believed to be quite simple,"
randma agreed slowly. The pony was tensing up again,
nd it was best to go on talking to it, about almost any-
ing at all. That always helped, even though the pony

knew her much too well by now to be really fooled by such tricks.

"Many very efficient life-forms aren't physically compli cated, you know," she went on, letting the sound of her voice ripple steadily into its mind. "Parasitical types, par ticularly. It's pretty certain, too, that the Halpa have the hive-mind class of intelligence, so what goes for the nerve systems of most of the ones they send through to us might be nothing much more than secondary reflex-transmitters. . . ."

Grimp stirred in his sleep at that point and grumbled. Grandma looked down at him. "You're sound asleep!" she told him severely, and he was again.

"You've got plans for that boy, haven't you?" the pony said without shifting its gaze from the hollow.

"I've had my eye on him," Grandma admitted, "and I've already recommended him to Headquarters for observation. But I'm not going to make up my mind about Grimp till next summer, when we've had more time to study him. Meanwhile, we'll see what he picks up naturally from the lortel in the way of telepathic communication and sensory extensions. I think Grimp's the kind we can use."

"He's all right," the pony agreed absently. "A bit murder ous, though, like most of you. . . ."

"He'll grow out of it!" Grandma said, a little annoyedly, for the subject of human aggressiveness was one she and the pony argued about frequently. "You can't hurry develop ments like that along too much. All of Noorhut should grow out of that stage, as a people, in another few hun dred years. They're about at the turning-point right now—"

Their heads came up together, then, as something very much like a big, dark rag of leather came fluttering up from the hollow and hung in the dark air above them. The representatives of the opposing powers that were meet ing on Noorhut that night took quiet stock of one another for a moment.

The Halpa was about six foot long and two wide, and con siderably less than an inch thick. It held its position in the air with a steady, rippling motion, like a bat the size of a

n. Then, suddenly, it extended itself with a snap, grow-
taut as a curved sail.

The pony snorted involuntarily. The apparently feature-
s shape in the air turned towards it and drifted a few
hes closer. When nothing more happened, it turned again
d fluttered quietly back down into the hollow.

"Could it tell I was scared?" the pony asked uneasily.

"You reacted just right," Grandma said soothingly.
tartled suspicion at first, and then just curiosity, and then
other start when it made that jump. It's about what
y'd expect from creatures that would be hanging around
hollow now. We're like cows to them. They can't tell
at things are by their looks, like we do—"

But her tone was thoughtful, and she was more shaken
n she would have cared to let the pony notice. There
d been something indescribably menacing and self-assured
the Halpa's gesture. Almost certainly, it had only been
ing to draw a reaction of hostile intelligence from them,
bing, perhaps, for the presence of weapons that might
dangerous to its kind.

But there was a chance—a tiny but appalling chance—
t the things *had* developed some drastically new form of
ack since their last break-through, and that they already
re in control of the situation. . . .

In which case, neither Grimp nor anyone else on Noor-
t would be doing any more growing-up after tomorrow.

Each of the eleven hundred and seventeen planets that
d been lost to the Halpa so far still traced a fiery, for-
dding orbit through space—torn back from the invaders
ly at the cost of depriving it, by humanity's own weap-
s, of the conditions any known form of life could
erate.

The possibility that this might also be Noorhut's future
l loomed as an ugly enormity before her for the past
r years. But of the nearly half a hundred worlds which
Halpa were found to be investigating through their de-
tor-globes as possible invasion points for this period, Noor-
: finally had been selected by Headquarters as the one
ere local conditions were most suited to meet them suc-
sfully. And that meant in a manner which must include

the destruction of their only real invasion weapon, the fab-
lous and mysterious Halpa transmitter. Capable as they u-
doubtedly were, they had shown in the past that they we-
able or willing to employ only one of those instrumen-
for each period of attack. Destroying the transmitter mea-
therefore that humanity would gain a few more centuri-
to figure out a way to get back at the Halpa before a ne-
attempt was made.

So on all planets but Noorhut the detector-globes ha-
been encouraged carefully to send back reports of a dange-
ously alert and well-armed population. On Noorhut, howeve-
they had been soothed along . . . and just as her hom-
planet had been chosen as the most favorable point of e-
counter, so was Erisa Wannattel herself selected as the age-
most suited to represent humanity's forces under the cond-
tions that existed there.

Grandma sighed gently and reminded herself again th-
Headquarters was as unlikely to miscalculate the overa-
probability of success as it was to select the wrong perso-
to achieve it. There was only the tiniest, the most theore-
ical, of chances that something might go wrong and th-
she would end her long career with the blundering murd-
of her own home-world.

But there was that chance.

"There seem to be more down there every minute!" th-
pony was saying.

Grandma drew a deep breath.

"Must be several thousand by now," she acknowledge-
"It's getting near breakthrough time, all right, but thos-
are only the advance forces." She added, "Do you notic-
anything like a glow of light down there, towards th-
center?"

The pony stared a moment. "Yes," it said. "But I woul-
have thought that was way under the red for you. Ca-
you see it?"

"No," said Grandma. "I get a kind of feeling, like heat-
That's the transmitter beginning to come through. I thin-
we've got them!"

The pony shifted its bulk slowly from side to side.

"Yes," it said resignedly, "or they've got us."

"Don't think about that," Grandma ordered sharply and umped one more mental lock shut on the foggy, dark rors that were curling and writhing under her conscious oughts, threatening to emerge at the last moment and ralyze her actions.

She had opened her black bag and was unhurriedly fitting gether something composed of a few pieces of wood and re, and a rather heavy, stiff spring. . . .

"Just be ready," she added.

"I've been ready for an hour," said the pony, shuffling feet unhappily.

They did no more talking after that. All the valley had come quiet about them. But slowly the hollow below was ing up with a black, stirring, slithering tide. Bits of it ttered up now and then like strips of black smoke, hovered ew yards above the mass and settled again.

Suddenly, down in the center of the hollow, there was nething else.

The pony had seen it first, Grandma Wannattel realized. was staring in that direction for almost a minute before e grew able to distinguish something that might have been group of graceful miniature spires. Semi-transparent in e darkness, four small domes showed at the corners, th a larger one in the center. The central one was about enty feet high and very slender.

The whole structure began to solidify swiftly. . . .

The Halpa Transmitter's appearance of crystalline slight-ss was perhaps the most mind-chilling thing about it. r it brought instantly a jarring sense of what must be ck distance beyond all distances, reaching back unimag-bly to its place of origin. In that unknown somewhere prodigiously talented and determined race of beings had ored for human centuries to prepare and point some pendous gun . . . and were able then to bridge the vast erval with nothing more substantial than this dark sliver glass that had come to rest suddenly in the valley of the nd.

But, of course, the Transmitter was all that was needed: deadly poison lay in a sluggish, almost inert mass about

it. Within minutes from now, it would waken to life, a
similar transmitters had wakened on other nights on tho⟨⟩
lost and burning worlds. And in much less than minutes a⟨⟩
ter that, the Halpa invaders would be hurled by their slend⟨⟩
machine to every surface section of Noorhut—no long⟨⟩
inert, but quickened into a ravening, almost indestructib⟨⟩
form of vampiric life, dividing and sub-dividing in its i⟨⟩
credibly swift cycle of reproduction, fastening to feed ane⟨⟩
growing and dividing again—

Spreading, at that stage, much more swiftly than it cou⟨⟩
be exterminated by anything but the ultimate weapons!

The pony stirred suddenly, and she felt the wave ⟨⟩
panic roll up in it.

"It's the Transmitter, all right," Grandma's thought reach⟨⟩
it quickly. "We've had two descriptions of it before. B⟨⟩
we can't be sure it's *here* until it begins to charge itse⟨⟩
Then it lights up—first at the edges, and then at the cente⟨⟩
Five seconds after the central spire lights up, it will be ene⟨⟩
gized too much to let them pull it back again. At lea⟨⟩
they couldn't pull it back after that, the last time th⟨⟩
were observed. And then we'd better be ready—"

The pony had been told all that before. But as it listen⟨⟩
it was quieting down again.

"And you're going to go on sleeping!" Grandma Wann⟨⟩
tel's thought told Grimp next. "No matter what you he⟨⟩
or what happens, you'll sleep on and know nothing at ⟨⟩
any more until I wake you up. . . ."

Light surged up suddenly in the Transmitter—first in
the four outer spires, and an instant later into the big centr⟨⟩
one, in a sullen red glow. It lit the hollow with a smok⟨⟩
glare. The pony took two startled steps backwards.

"Five seconds to go!" whispered Grandma's thought. S⟨⟩
reached into her black bag again and took out a small plast⟨⟩
ball. It reflected the light from the hollow in dull crims⟨⟩
gleamings. She let it slip down carefully inside the shaftli⟨⟩
frame of the gadget she had put together of wood and wir⟨⟩
It clicked into place there against one end of the cor⟨⟩
pressed spring.

Down below, they lay now in a blanket fifteen feet thi⟨⟩

ver the wet ground, like big, black, water-sogged leaves
wept up in circular piles about the edges of the hollow.
he tops and sides of the piles were stirring and shivering
nd beginning to slide down toward the Transmitter.

". . . five, and go!" Grandma said aloud. She raised
ne wooden catapult to her shoulder.

The pony shook its blunt-horned head violently from side
o side, made a strangled, bawling sound, surged forward
nd plunged down the steep side of the hollow in a thunder-
ng rush.

Grandma aimed carefully and let go.

The blanket of dead-leaf things was lifting into the air
head of the pony's ground-shaking approach in a weight-
ess, silent swirl of darkness which instantly blotted both
ne glowing Transmitter and the pony's shape from sight.
he pony roared once as the blackness closed over it. A
econd later, there was a crash like the shattering of a
undred-foot mirror—and at approximately the same mo-
nent. Grandma's plastic ball exploded somewhere in the
enter of the swirling swarm.

Cascading fountains of white fire filled the whole of the
ollow. Within the fire, a dense mass of shapes fluttered
nd writhed frenziedly like burning rags. From down where
ne fire boiled fiercest rose continued sounds of brittle sub-
ances suffering enormous violence. The pony was
ampling the ruined Transmitter, making sure of its de-
truction.

"Better get out of it!" Grandma shouted anxiously. "What's
eft of that will all melt now anyway!"

She didn't know whether it heard her or not. But a few
econds later, it came pounding up the side of the hollow
gain. Blazing from nose to rump, it tramped past Grand-
na, plunged through the meadow behind her, shedding white
neets of fire that exploded the marsh grass in its tracks,
nd hurled itself headlong into the pond it had selected
reviously. There was a great splash, accompanied by sharp
issing noises. Pond and pony vanished together under bil-
wing clouds of steam.

"That was pretty hot!" its thought came to Grandma.

She drew a deep breath.

"Hot as anything that ever came out of a volcano!" she affirmed. "If you'd played around in it much longer, you'd have fixed up the village with roasts for a year."

"I'll just stay here for a while, till I've cooled off a bit," said the pony.

Grandma found something strangling her then, and discovered it was the lortel's tail. She unwound it carefully. But the lortel promptly reanchored itself with all four hands in her hair. She decided to leave it there. It seemed badly upset.

Grimp, however, slept on. It was going to take a little maneuvering to get him back into the village undetected before morning, but she would figure that out by and by. A steady flow of cool night-air was being drawn past them into the hollow now and rising out of it again in boiling, vertical columns of invisible heat. At the bottom of the deluxe blaze she'd lit down there, things still seemed to be moving about—but very slowly. The Halpa were tough organisms, all right, though not nearly so tough, when you heated them up with a really good incendiary, as were the natives of Treebel.

She would have to make a final check of the hollow around dawn, of course, when the ground should have cooled off enough to permit it—but her century's phase of the Halpa War did seem to be over. The defensive part of it, at any rate—

Wet, munching sounds from the pond indicated the pony felt comfortable enough by now to take an interest in the parboiled vegetation it found floating around it. Everything had turned out all right.

So she settled down carefully on her back in the long marsh grass without disturbing Grimp's position too much, and just let herself faint for a while.

By sunrise, Grandma Wannattel's patent-medicine trailer was nine miles from the village and rolling steadily southwards up the valley road through the woods. As usual, she was departing under a cloud.

Grimp and the policeman had showed up early to warn her. The Guardian was making use of the night's various

precedented disturbances to press through a vote on a
blic Menace charge against Grandma in the village; and
ce everybody still felt rather excited and upset, he had
good chance just now of getting a majority.

Grimp had accompanied her far enough to explain that
is state of affairs wasn't going to be permanent. He had
all worked out.

Runny's new immunity to hay-fever had brought him
d the pretty Vellit to a fresh understanding overnight;
ey were going to get married five weeks from now. As a
arried man, Runny would then be eligible for the post
  Village Guardian at the harvest elections—and be-
een Grimp's cousins and Vellit's cousins, Runny's backers
ould just about control the vote. So when Grandma
t around to visiting the valley again next summer, she
edn't worry any more about police interference or official
approval. . . .

Grandma had nodded approvingly. That was about the
nd of neighborhood politics she'd begun to play herself
Grimp's age. She was pretty sure by now that Grimp
as the one who eventually would become her successor,
d the guardian not only of Noorhut and the star-system
which Noorhut belonged, but of a good many other star-
stems besides. With careful schooling, he ought to be just
out ready for the job by the time she was willing, finally,
retire.

An hour after he had started back to the farm, looking
ddenly a little forlorn, the trailer swung off the valley
ad into a narrow forest path. Here the pony lengthened its
ide, and less than five minutes later they entered a curv-
g ravine, at the far end of which lay something that
rimp would have recognized instantly, from his one visit
the nearest port city, as a small spaceship.

A large round lock opened soundlessly in its side as they
proached. The pony came to stop. Grandma got down from
e driver's seat and unhitched it. The pony walked into the
ck, and the trailer picked its wheels off the ground and
ated in after it. Grandma Wannattel walked in last, and
e lock closed quietly on her heels.

The ship lay still a moment longer. Then it was sud-

denly gone. Dead leaves went dancing for a while abo
the ravine, disturbed by the breeze of its departure.

In a place very far away—so far that neither Grim
nor his parents nor anyone in the village except the schoo
teacher had ever heard of it—a set of instruments bega
signalling for attention. Somebody answered them.

Grandma's voice announced distinctly:

"This is Zone Agent Wannattel's report of the succes:
ful conclusion of the Halpa operation on Noorhut—"

High above Noorhut's skies, eight great ships swung i
stantly out of their watchful orbits about the planet an
flashed off again into the blackness of the boundless spac
that was their sea and their home.